The Mirror and the Mage

A novel of ancient Rome

by

D. W. FRAUENFELDER

BREAKFAST WITH PANDORA BOOKS

In association with

True North Writers & Publishers Co-operative

Durham, North Carolina

Also by D. W. Frauenfelder

Skater in a Strange Land
The Skater and the Saint

::Salvete - Greetings::

HAEC EST FABULA VERA AUT SIMILLIMA VERI

Based on a true story

MAGISTRIS CARISSIMIS

To my teachers

CONTENTS

i

::I::

"You can't do it," said Arruns.

"I can so do it," said Lucius.

"I think he can do it," said Publius. "So why don't you, Lucius?"

Lucius of the Roman household of Junius considered his answer. He didn't have long-- soon it would be dark and the opportunity would be lost.

Lucius looked out at the swift-running waters of the Tiber River and said, "I'll not only do it; you will see me do it. Before the sun sets, I will have swum the river and greeted you at the foot of the Sublician Bridge, on Tiber's further side."

The threesome scrambled down the overgrown bank, kicking away acorns and raising dust as they went. It was the solstice, the eve of summer, and the cicadas sang in the holm oaks and poplars. The smell of the river came up sweet and enticing through the bone-dry air. The setting sun threw a purple stripe over the surface of the moving water. The boys' uncut curls blazed as the warm breeze unfurled them in

1

strands.

At the edge of the water-- a rocky bank in between stands of reeds that grew well out toward the current-- a dragonfly buzzed through their midst, floated, hesitated, and was gone. Green scum floated in the shallows, but within a stone's throw the river was troubled with eddies and ripples.

"It is not that deep here," said Publius, throwing a skinny arm out at the Tiber. He was tall and narrow-faced and when he took off his shirt you could see his ribs. Not because he didn't eat; he belonged to the house of Valerius, a noble Roman family, and he ate better than nearly all Romans. "You could probably touch all the way across."

"That is not true," said Arruns. He would have been as skinny as Publius if he spent more time outside. But as the son of King Tarquin, his tutors too often kept him occupied with the study of statecraft. "We had a rainy winter, and the river is still well in spate. You know that, Publius Valerius. You spent most of it inside coughing out demons from your chest!"

"Here are the rules, Lucius Junius," said Publius in his important voice. He was hoping the king would invite him to be a *haruspex*, an Etruscan prophet and soothsayer, so he was in the habit of announcing important things. "You must swim across the Tiber. You must do it on your own with no help from boats, floating logs, or prayers to gods or river spirits."

This last he said with great seriousness, for he was a great believer in river spirits.

"You may not rest on the Tiber Island, or walk from one side of the island to the other in order to make your way easier. And you must be across the river before sunset, and at the Sublician Bridge, or we will not acknowledge your feat among the best boys of Rome."

Lucius nodded. To be acknowledged as a swimmer of the River Tiber before the age of fourteen was rare and glorious. It ensured that you would be picked by the king to be in the Etruscan army of Rome. And tomorrow was his birthday: he would be fourteen, he would have his locks cut, and he would be picked as a warrior, or (what his father wanted) as priest.

"Do you solemnly swear upon the genius of your ancestors that you will not invoke the name of a god to help you?"

"I do swear it," Lucius.

Lucius shook the boys' hands, took off his tunic and sandals, leaving on only his leggings. Publius gathered up the bundle of things and promised to deliver it at the end of the swim. Then, with a final wave and farewell-- *Valete!* in Latin, and both boys saying *Vale!* back to him, he waded into the sacred depths. It had long been told among the Romans who lived on seven hills near this life-giving river that there was a god in the waves, Father Tiber, Tiberinus, an old, mysterious spirit. Unlike many of his family and friends, Lucius seldom felt any presence in the river when they walked down from the hills to give the customary monthly and yearly offerings.

But now, as he waded on the gravelly bed through reeds that brushed against his legs, the water almost up to his neck, Lucius thought he felt a hand underneath his feet, encouraging him to thrust himself forward, and to kick his legs, and cut the surface of the river with hands rigid like knife-blades. The hand seemed to carry his feet higher, and to give him a push on his way.

Lucius lowered his head, dunked it underwater, and began to swim. It was warmer than he had expected, and for a

3

moment he thought that swimming the River Tiber at summer solstice would be one of the easier things he had done. The river was not wide, and if still, could be swum in no time.

The question was the current. At certain times of the year, when the river was rising to the top of its banks with runoff from rain and snowfall upstream, anyone trying to swim it would be carried off and his body found miles downstream, near the harbor of Ostia. In early fall, before the rains began, or in drought time, it could be walked all the way across.

Now, at the beginning of summer, it was still fast in places, but a strong boy, or a lucky one, might dare to swim it.

Lucius was neither weak nor unlucky-- so he thought-- and as his strokes cut the water, he could see the other side, thickly overgrown with poplars and reeds, and had no fear.

But then he got into the main current of the river, and the hand that had lifted him up so easily before now began to tug at him, to carry him downstream, and to whisper into his ear, "No further across will you go."

He treaded water for a moment, stuck his head up, and caught sight of the Tiber Island. Of course he could not be carried that far, and certainly not as far downstream as the Sublician Bridge, could he?

But the river still tugged at him, and the distance to the other bank was no less.

He tried to stroke again, and found it hard going, and for the first time his arms and legs began to ache.

For the briefest of instants he considered swimming back, but he knew he had come too far. He had to break through the primary current of the river. There would be stiller water near the other bank.

The Tiber Island loomed close, and he might make it there with a great effort. The boys would not see him if he stayed on the further side of the island, caught his breath, and then swam out again.

But Lucius had sworn to swim the river on his own.

The island passed by, and as the sun appeared again just above the treetops, Lucius gave another effort, thrashing over the ripples and eddies. He looked up, and thought the trees and reeds on the other side looked bigger, but couldn't be sure.

The posts of the bridge were looming closer. Lucius was now too weak to push his way out of the current before he went underneath it. The posts were close together, and the current heavy and high as it churned by. He would have to maneuver between them to avoid being brained in the head.

Lucius kicked toward the middle of the opening of two beams, but it was no use. The tug of the river god was too great. He headed straight for an enormous, battered post near the center of the bridge.

He caught sight of his friends, looking down from the railing in horror, just as he was sucked underwater.

Lucius Junius could see nothing, blinking in the near-dark, and felt nothing, until his hip hit something hard, and he bounced away; he coughed and swallowed water as he screamed in pain.

Spinning end over end, Lucius knew not whether he was near the bottom or the surface of the water. The river god had him in his fist, and there was nothing he could do.

His limbs relaxed, and bursts of light went in his mind's eye. He heard his father's words filling his ears like the Tiber was now filling his lungs.

"Rejoice, son," said Marcus Junius the Elder. "You will be priest of the holy shrine established by Numa. You will watch over the sacred bark with the first signs of the Latin language incised upon them."

A fate worse than death, Lucius had thought at the time.

But when Father Tiber did push the boy up to the surface again, and he coughed, and his lungs took in air rather than water, Lucius screamed to himself, *I will* not *die! If the priesthood is what the gods want me to have, then have it I shall! This I do solemnly vow!*

He had no strength to swim, but let the current take him, and it naturally migrated toward the other bank. When he was almost in the evening shade of a holm oak's branches, he gave a last, desperate stroke, and found himself in still waters. Kicking, then testing for the bottom of the river, he found his way into the reed beds, and before long was lying on stones, still coughing, with his bruised hip smarting, and his arms and legs as heavy as pea bean mush.

The thick crowns of the poplars hid the sun-- it must have been nearly gone-- and Lucius still had a long walk to the Sublician Bridge in order to claim his prize, his glory among the best boys of the Roman city.

But now he felt nothing but shame. He dragged himself to his feet, made his way up the slope to a path that paralleled a stone wall. He walked along in the twilight next to a grove of fig trees, dripping water from his long, shaggy hair and soggy breeches.

He passed a barn where swallows were screeching in the eaves, and the sweet smell of the river in the dusty, dry air came to him again. Suddenly, he felt completely calm and at ease, and he raised his weary arms to the sky in thanks to the god that saved him.

"It is after sunset. I have lost my challenge," he would say to his friends. "I will be a priest of Numa Pompilius. I will not be a warrior."

He met no one on the path, seeing only a pigsty where fat porkers feasting on acorns grunted their greeting.

The first folk he saw were his two friends, meeting him at the Bridge.

"Thank Tiber," said Publius. "I thought surely you were dead!"

"You have won out," said Arruns. "The sun is still in the sky! It is the longest day of the year."

"But--" Lucius protested. He turned to the west. The sun was like a great flatbread on a dusky cooking stone.

"You are a man," said Arruns, taking Lucius by the shoulders. "You will be a great warrior in the army of King Tarquin the Proud."

::II::

The boys half-walked, half-ran across the bridge, for the watches on duty were closing the gate on the other side of the river for the night.

"Lucius Junius has swum the Tiber," called Arruns to the young men who manned the wooden palisade. "He will be a great warrior."

"By my genius," said one of the guards, "if Lucius Junius is a warrior, then I am an acorn in a pig's belly."

"I guess that is why you stink so badly," said Publius.

The guard raised his spear as if to cast it, and they sprinted away, laughing.

Lucius could not speak. He had vowed to be a priest. He was positive the sun had set. But it had not. The longest day of the year!

All along the Via, the main street of Rome, wending between the Capitoline and Palatine hills, the people were gathering for the celebration of the summer solstice. There would be feasts and games all night long, and in the morning the new recruits to the army would be announced.

Only the brightest stars blazed above, but Lucius' eyes were dazzled by the many torches set up along the Via and carried by young men eager to organize foot and horse races. The smells of meat cooking-- sausages especially, but also whole pigs and sheep turned on spits-- filled the air, along with the smoke of the wood fires which lay under the meat.

Lucius felt a tug on his tunic. He was still shivery from his swim, and the evening breeze felt colder than it would have otherwise, but at least the top of his tunic was dry.

The tugger was Demetria, nearly thirteen-year old girl and constant troublemaker. She was the daughter of a Greek trader who had set himself up in Rome selling perfumed olive oil. He was wealthy, but he still had his daughters stay at home to spin wool. Demetria sneaked out as often as possible, and was always punished for it, but not enough to keep her from sneaking out again.

"Lucius, where have you been? Your brother is looking all over for you!"

In addition to being a troublemaker, Demetria was in everyone's business. She knew the news before anyone else. And since she had lived in Rome nearly all her life, she spoke Latin perfectly.

"What is this? You're soaked all over. Don't tell me you dunked yourself in the Tiber River with these good-for-nothings!" And she tossed her thick black curls and laughed her troublemaker's laugh.

Arruns said, "Lucius swam the Tiber and will be a warrior for the army of King Tarquin the Proud. Now get back to your spinning, you wooly-haired little Greek brat."

Demetria ignored Arruns and instead turned to Lucius with wide eyes. "Does the great man speak the truth? You swam the Tiber?"

"Go tell the world, Demetria," said Publius. "We are convening the assembly of the best boys of Rome to announce Lucius' feat. Then we will present him before the king of Rome himself."

"It's not so hard to swim the Tiber," Demetria said. "I could do it myself."

"We will throw you in over the bridge," said Arruns. "Then we will see how long it takes you to drown."

"Tell me, Lucius," she said, and her eyes lost their troublemaker's light. "You're really going to be a warrior, not a priest of Numa?"

Lucius still could not say anything. He opened his mouth, but nothing came out.

Demetria stopped in her tracks. "Lucius?" she said.

"Good riddance," said Arruns, as they left her behind.

Lucius wished he had been able to say something to Demetria. She was not only a troublemaker. From an early age, she had also been a playmate; she had sneaked out of her house and they had played priest and priestess, pulling bark off of trees and making up their own secret language, scratching signs into the bark as the ancient Romans had done, and making offerings of rye seed and caterpillars to an imaginary being they called the God of Everything.

On fine days when the women sat and spun outside, Demetria and Lucius listened to her aunt tell tales of the hero Hercules and his impossible feats-- battling the Hydra, cleaning the Augean Stables, defeating Cacus, the monster who lived in

Rome before it was Rome.

As they grew older, Demetria would dream aloud of how one day Lucius would really be a priest, and she would be his handmaid, and they would learn the secret lore of Rome together, the ancient wisdom of Numa Pompilius.

Lately, as Lucius came closer to manhood, they spent less and less time together. He practiced athletics and swordsmanship with his friends, and Demetria, having become an expert spinner of wool and a moneymaker for her family, could not sneak away from her work as often.

To Lucius, what they had done seemed to him childish, even crazy. Greek girls and Roman boys should not play together.

Nevertheless, they had.

Now, as Demetria stood there with the torchlight brightening and darkening her face as the flames flared or died, she called to him one last time: "*Arana Atana.*"

The phrase was from their secret language. It meant, "Farewell, my friend."

The boy council of Rome met in the crook of a hill known as the Esquiline. Here was a grassy meadow once used as grazing for cattle, but the herders had moved farther out of town into wider, flatter lands. Farmers, too, had tried to use the land, but hadn't the patience to pull out all the heavy stones that made plowing difficult.

On these stones the boys sat, and the speaker took his place at the foot of the slope. Only those from the most important families of Rome were allowed to speak, oldest to youngest in order. The leader was always the eldest boy not yet fourteen years old and not wearing the *toga virilis*, the robe of manhood.

That person tonight was Publius, a few weeks younger than the newly fourteen-year old Lucius.

News had traveled fast. There were already about two-dozen youths sitting on rocks in ones and twos, with boys too young to be members standing to the side.

Publius could hardly quiet the boys, for tonight was one of the most exciting in all the year, and now, with the rumors about Lucius, and Lucius himself there, still shivering in wet breeches, there was even more to talk about.

Nevertheless, when Publius shouted "*Salvete!*" "Greetings!" from a great stone at the foot of the slope, all the boys rose and shouted, "*Salve et tu!*" back to him, and every boy left off from chatter.

"Hear me, boys of Rome," said Publius. "We have a new candidate for the army of King Tarquin: Lucius of the house of Junius."

This set the council into an uproar; for some time Publius could not make himself heard.

"As leader of the boy council of Rome, I say that we present Lucius before the king, tonight, all agreeing, every one of us."

More chattering, but then the next oldest boy stood up, Sextus Tarquinius, the other son of the king.

"Lucius Junius is from a family of priests," Sextus said. "He is not allowed to become a warrior."

"But he has swum the Tiber!" yelled Arruns.

"You are out of turn," said Publius, turning to Arruns, who was a year younger than Sextus. "Quiet down."

"Is it true that he has swum the Tiber?" someone yelled.

"You are out of turn as well," said Publius.

The next in line, Tullius, a Roman, said, "His brother Marcus has become a warrior. So he can as well."

Publius said, "This was against his parents' wishes," and most of the council nodded in agreement.

"Who saw him swim the Tiber?" asked someone. Arruns raised his hand, but Publius waved his hands for quiet.

The next speaker, Ceflans, an Etruscan, said, "If he has swum the Tiber, he is allowed to go into the army. Does he wish to go?"

Publius pointed at Lucius, who came forward. His ears were buzzing. It felt as if he were a ghost. He could not feel his feet, his arms, or hands. He still could not speak.

"Is he cursed?" Sextus said to the boy sitting next to him. "He has not said a word yet, and he is usually the one who speaks the most."

"For sure," said the other. "Do you remember how he put stones in his mouth one time to practice for his speech here? This is a god's doing, I think."

"What say you, Lucius, what say you?" They all yelled at him.

"I wish it," Lucius finally blurted, and Publius raised his arm for him. He never said what he wished, but all took it for his commitment to the Roman army. Everyone yelled and screamed at once, and Publius couldn't get them to quiet down. After a time, some of the boys approached Lucius, and lifted him onto their shoulders.

"To Tarquin, to the king," they all shouted.

Lucius looked about him. It appeared he was to be a warrior.

But then he saw Marcus.

::III::

When the boys caught sight of Marcus Junius, the older brother of Lucius, to be seventeen years old that fall, the entire group fell silent. Lucius slid off the shoulders of his friends.

Marcus was tall and slender, his expression noble and confident, and most of the time carefree. But now his jaw was set and his black eyes lidded over with concern. He had always seemed tall to Lucius, and now more than ever as he shook his head and left his hand on his hip, his tunic flapping in the warm breeze.

Marcus' voice rang out. "Is it true what they say?"

Lucius shrugged without wanting to. He didn't want to shrug his shoulders in front of a warrior of Rome, as if he were a shamed child.

"Tell me, Lucius," said Marcus. "Did you swim the river?"

"Yes, brother," he said.

Marcus smiled widely. He took his brother by the shoulders, and then lifted him up in a great hug. "You great fool! By Quirinus, I'm proud of you, you stupid brute! Nine

14

times out of a ten a boy is drowned at this time of year. What spirit possessed you, brother? And now you will have Mother and Father to answer to. By my genius, brother, it was not an easy thing to swim the Tiber, but our parents?"

"But now I will be a warrior, like you."

At this, Marcus let go of Lucius, put him back on the ground, and some of the glower came back into his face. "That is just the point, Lucius. There are only two sons of Marcus Junius the Elder. One is already a warrior. The other must be a priest, to keep the lore alive. The king has made me go into the army, but you--" he took the arm of Lucius and squeezed. "You are the last hope."

Lucius and Marcus met Mother and Father in the courtyard fronting the house of King Tarquin, its low wall shaded by Italian pines. It had been paved in stones of tufa, the soft volcanic rock that was plentiful near Rome, and its edges were of marble imported from Greece. This is where Tarquin made his judgments, and anything decreed on the pavement was binding as law.

The Junius family stood on the pavement as King Tarquin the Proud emerged from the front door of his house, walking with attendants on his left and right. A chair was set up for him on the pavement, and he looked over all his assembled people.

"Don't speak," said Father behind his hand.

Mother put her arms around Lucius and her tear-stained cheeks against his. "Lucius!" she whispered into his ear. "Lucius, my son. By Juno, my son."

"Shhh," said Father. "Compose yourself."

The king stood and extended his hand to Father. "Marcus Junius the Elder, my friend," he said. "Your son is safe, thank

Father Tiber."

Tarquin then looked out at the crowd in front of him. The whole pavement was filled, and there were more coming. "This is an auspicious night," he said, loud enough so that the crowd quieted to hear him. "We have news that one of the noblest boys of Rome is presenting himself for admission into the army of Etruria. Who is this boy? Let him come forward."

Mother held tightly to Lucius, and Father extended his arm in front of Lucius.

"No boy of Rome presents himself," said Father. "No one comes forward."

"Explain, Marcus," said the King.

Father spoke clearly and with great force, so that even those on the margins of the pavement could hear. "The household of Junius has been, since the time of Numa Pompilius, the guardians of the ancient lore of the Romans. My son is dedicated to this knowledge."

"But did I not hear," Tarquin broke in, his voice equally loud and commanding, "that this boy swam the Tiber before sunset on the longest day of the year? My own son swears it."

Father nodded. "Let him so swear. It does not change this boy's destiny. He is my son. He is a Roman. He will guard the scrolls."

"But he is Etruscan," called someone in the crowd.

Father scowled, turning to see who had spoken. Lucius did not turn, but he knew that whoever said it was speaking the truth. Mother, Junia Tarquinia, was the granddaughter of the first Etruscan king of Rome, Tarquinius Priscus, and the king himself her brother. Father was of Roman blood.

Father said darkly, "He is Roman."

"The Etruscans reckon lineage from the mother's side," said Tarquin.

"And the Romans from the father's," said Father. He set his jaw, much as the younger Marcus had done with Lucius.

The crowd went into an uproar. No one noticed Lucius leaving the pavement for a field behind it. He found a stray brick in the waving brown grass. He brought it into the center of the pavement, and he cast it down hard, so that it smashed into two pieces.

"I have vowed it," he said, and for a moment it was as if he was standing on the cliff of a great mountain, and was about to fling himself from it, and fall forever.

Now no one spoke on either side. All eyes were on Lucius.

"I vowed that..." He paused, and looked up at his father, and his brother, and he spoke the words he knew he had to say. "When I was in the Tiber, and about to go to my ancestors, I vowed to whatever god saved me that I would be a priest of Numa. I cannot go back on my vow."

Everyone gasped.

"Why do you say this now?" said Tarquin. "Are you doing it to please your father?"

"No," said Lucius. "What I have vowed, I have vowed."

"Very well," said Tarquin after the crowd quieted again. "Let him go to the babbling priest of Latium. But I, King Tarquin, decree this: that in a year's time, this boy will return here and we will make prophecy by the *haruspices* of Etruria: shall he waste his life guarding nonsense, or will he join my army to be a great hero of the Etruscan nation? But forever afterward, whatever choice be made by the gods, this young man shall be called Brutus, the slow-witted, for though he swam the Tiber before sunset on the longest day of the year, and had the right to be a great general, yet he vowed instead to guard scratchings on plane-tree bark."

The king stood up from his chair, shook hands with Father, and went back into his house.

"The night is yours, Lucius Junius Brutus," said Marcus, after a hundred Romans had congratulated Lucius. "One great and glorious night before you must go on to the babbler."

"Have I chosen wrong, brother?" said Lucius.

"No, indeed, little brother," said Marcus. He laughed and said, "It may have been the vow of a slow-witted boy, but it was right to fulfill it."

"You laugh at me," said Lucius. "As if I were a child!"

"No, not at all," said Marcus. "Tarquin knows our family is a rival to his in the kingship. He wants to keep an eye on us. Already I am in the brigade of his army with his most loyal followers. He thinks I can do nothing against him. But with the priest of Numa, you will be out of sight. This is not to Tarquin's liking. But for our family, it is good."

"What good?"

"Don't let it trouble you, Lucius. You will be called on when the time is right. But keep practicing your swordsmanship, if the priest of Numa allow it." And Marcus laughed again, as if he had said they were all going honeycomb-hunting on the longest night of the year.

The festival went by in a blur of light and smoke. Lucius would never forget it, but then again he would never be able to recall exactly what had happened. For in all the feasting and footraces, all the dancing and music, all the girls who gave him goodbye kisses, and boys' farewells echoing in his ears, even in the ceremony where all his long hair was sacrificed to Mars and he was given the toga of manhood, he could pick out no one moment that did not melt into the next.

He never met Demetria that night. He never asked about her, and no one mentioned her. Of all the people to say farewell to, the goodbye of Demetria was the one he most coveted. But as the sun rose on the next day, and he and his family entered the sacred grove of Numa Pompilius, Lucius knew that Demetria had already said her farewell: *Arana Atana*.

Not saying anything back to her may have been the most slow-witted thing he had done that day.

::IV::

Lucius Junius Brutus was either lost or close to it.

The day had begun well enough. The Junius family walked together in the waning darkness, along a straight path to the sacred grove, where, so the story went, the great Numa Pompilius, priest-king of Rome, had met Egeria, an immortal lady who had given him sacred knowledge and told him to preserve it.

Here, Mother, Father, and Marcus had said their final goodbyes, as the dawn reddened the eastern horizon, and Father had prayed a prayer in the stillness of the oak trees.

"Go with your genius," said Father. "You have done well. Safe journey."

Soon, the sun was up and yellow-gold. Lucius followed the path his father pointed out, and after a much-needed nap on his cloak under a tree next to a grassy field full of lowing Roman cows, a meal of flatbread, cheese, and an apple, and more walking (much more), the sun was at his back, tickling his newly-bare neck, and there was no indication when his road would be finished.

"It is a long way," Father had said, "but stay to the path. Once you come to the ridge with the crooked fig tree, you are almost there, and someone will come and fetch you to the priest."

Lucius had come to several ridges--or what he considered to be ridges--and several crooked fig trees, but never a ridge with a fig tree. If he didn't find the shrine before sunset, he would either have to sleep under the stars or walk much of the night to return home.

The path had taken him into a hill country of scrub oak, pine, and thorn bushes interspersed with aromatic mustard, juniper and rosemary. Thickets of blackberry, not yet ripe, grew amidst wild vegetables: sorrel and mallow. These last two were things Lucius could eat if he had to spend the night outside and didn't mind a stomachache, but he had not come upon any spring for a long time and was thirsty. He had met no one on the path and even the birds had deserted him. The only sound was the sleepy cicadas.

Lucius had heard tales that gods visited those who ventured out into such wilderness. Shepherds especially were prone to visions, and afterwards, often became poets.

Lucius was not the type to hear voices. Others claimed to have heard the spirits of woods and springs, but Lucius had spent much of his life in the noisy Forum, the center of town, where the only voices were those of men saying things they (and sometimes, only they) considered important. But now, as Lucius came to the top of a ridge, leaned on an old fig tree trunk, hatcheted clean at torso level, and wondered for the seventeenth time that hour where he might find his spring, he distinctly heard a voice in his head.

"Do you know where you're going?"

Lucius blinked and looked behind him. The path stretched back, rocky and downhill. He turned. In front of him the path wended its way into a grove of low-hanging oaks.

"Do you really want to go forward? It could be dangerous."

Was it a god who spoke? The first statement had seemed to come from everywhere. But now, Lucius' keen ear told him the words had come from the path to the oaks.

"Who's that?" said Lucius, turning toward the sound. He had wanted to be commanding, but his tone was unsure.

The voice took on some of the courage that Lucius lacked. "If I were you, I'd turn baaa-ack." It was a kind of threat. But whoever was the owner, the voice was not particularly menacing. In fact, it was high-pitched, even squeaky.

"Show yourself!" Lucius said, stronger now.

"Do you not fear the gods?"

"I might fear you if I could see you."

A slight pause before the reply: "Well, I can't be seen. I'm a genius."

Now Lucius was even more suspicious. He had been taught that the only genius he'd be able to hear was his own: the divine spirit of himself, his guardian.

"Are you my genius?"

An even longer pause: "Well yes, maybe I am."

Lucius caught a flash of movement in a nearby oak tree. He peered through the leaves. Someone was lying on a long, thick horizontal branch. The someone was dressed in a dull, almost colorless linen tunic that blended in with the tawny grass growing next to and behind the tree. His skin was wrinkled and leathery like the bark of the tree.

"Show yourself, genius! I can see you there in the tree."

The genius scrambled toward the trunk of the tree and hid behind it. "I don't think you can see me."

"Well, see you or not, I'm not frightened of you and I need to be on my way to the shrine of Numa."

"Shrine of Numa? Why are you looking for that?"

"I am to be the new priest in the shrine, but I think I am lost. My father told me to look for a crooked fig tree at the top of a ridge, but I have found no such tree on any ridge I have topped."

The genius stepped out from behind the tree and into the path. It was an old man with limbs as spindly as an old fig's. He pointed. "You may not see that fig tree, but you have found it."

Lucius looked about him. "Found it?"

"It's the very tree you were leaning on."

Lucius almost jumped. "But it's not crooked at all."

"That's because we cut it down. It was rotten!"

Lucius wanted to laugh but all he could do was stand there with his mouth open.

Instead the genius laughed. "You look like Janus with his door shut on both faces!"

Since Janus was the twin-faced god of open doors, Lucius understood he must have looked surprised indeed, if not angry and a bit cheated. "Who are you really, cutter of fig trees?" he said.

"Forgive me, future priest of Numa. My name is Logophilus, and I am the assistant of the priest of Numa, Publius Litterarius."

"Assistant?" said Lucius.

"Yes, assistant, not slave. I am here with the priest on my own. No one forced me! For I love the writings of Numa."

"Those old scratchings on plane-tree bark?"

"They are more than scratchings, young master. But you will see. Tell me, what is your name, if you are so disdainful of the holy grammar?"

"I am Lucius Junius who is called Brutus by the king of Rome."

"He who is slow-witted shall learn letters? Now I've heard everything. Well, come. We have not had a visitor for many months. You must meet the priest."

Lucius followed Logophilus into the oak grove. Before long they were descending into a shady glen. Green grass grew up, and wild flowers, where the trees let in light. At the foot of the glen, a stony brook ran through, swift and clear.

"This goes finally to Father Tiber," said Logophilus. "Up above are the spring, and the spirit. To cross, we must thank the spirit."

"I am thirsty," said Lucius.

"Then drink now," said Logophilus. "For when we see the priest, he is liable to talk long."

Lucius bent down and scooped handfuls of water into his mouth. It was the best he had ever tasted, and not just because he was thirsty.

"There is something in this," Lucius said, splashing his hot face with the water. All at once he felt calm, satisfied, and completely without fear.

"There is something in everything if you look for it," said Logophilus, and he said a word of thanks to the spirit of the spring.

"What was there in your voice?" said Lucius as they resumed their downhill walk. "At first it seemed to come from all around me. Do you fool many people with it?"

"Ah," said Logophilus. "You will learn to do this and much more."

Lucius was about to be annoyed by the old man's mysterious answers, but he forgot to be when he caught sight of a clearing with a hut, a woodpile, and a fenced vegetable garden. The whole was not much bigger than the pavement of King Tarquin, and surrounded by wild olive, laurel, and myrtle trees.

"Is this where the priest lives?"

"Ah, no," said Logophilus. "This is the *casula*-- where I live."

They crossed a bare patch in front of the *casula*, and a dog lying near the threshold of the house pricked up its ears. It was yellow, with a blackish face and eyes, and it fell in step with them as they went into the trees again, along a path that was dirt for the first few steps, but then became stone stairs.

"Up," said Logophilus. The dog did not follow, but sat down and whined, opening its mouth and curling its long tongue.

They were next to a ridge of gray stone veined with silver. Lucius' legs, already tired, began to ache as he ascended the carved stairs. There was the sound of water, and around a curve came a waterfall, tumbling down the ridge and making a clear curtain in front of them.

"So much water," Lucius said. "We are in a place of gods."

"Inside," said Logophilus. "Through the curtain."

Lucius pushed his way through. The water was cold and gave him a brief shock, but then he was inside, and a cave opened up, mossy and cool. A few steps within, a rug hung from a rod in a hole in the cave.

"Beware," said Logophilus. "He is not...ah, shall we say, safe."

"What do you mean?"

But Logophilus did not have to answer. There was a great whoosh of air, the rug flew up, and both Lucius and Logophilus were thrown from their feet.

They had hardly picked up their heads from the wet stone when the dog trotted out of the threshold, its tail wagging, and stopped in front of Lucius.

"Great priest-- is a dog?" Lucius managed. His elbow was smarting where it had hit the cave floor.

Logophilus said nothing, just wheezed and rubbed his hip. In the threshold there appeared a man, no taller than Lucius himself, leaning on a walking stick made of bone. He was bald and clean-shaven, and around his left eye he was tattooed with blue concentric circles. He might have been a hundred years old, or fifty. It was impossible to tell.

"Don't mind Kaneesh," said the man, his voice clear and rounded, like a much younger man's. "She knows more than one way to enter the Caves of Egeria, and she does not like to get wet."

"Master," said Logophilus. "You perfected your grammar?"

"It is never perfect, dear Logophilus," said the man. He waved the cane at Lucius. "You can stand, young man?"

"Yes, father," said Lucius.

"Then do so. I am Publius Litterarius by name," he said.

"Those who know me call me Glyph."

What type of name is Glyph? Lucius wondered. Certainly not a Roman name.

"Let us take a meal, Logo," said Glyph. "It's been a long day, and that is the third time the rug has gone flying."

At the word "meal," the dog barked, and panted. It went back through the threshold of the cave and disappeared. Logophilus turned and went back through the curtain of water, leaving Glyph and Lucius alone.

"I am no Etruscan seer, but I think you must be the son of Marcus Junius the Elder," said Glyph.

"I am Lucius, called Brutus, the son of Marcus. How do you know me?"

"Because a long time ago, your father stood before me, the same age as you. It is as if he is here now, and no time has passed. You are tall and slender as he was, with the same heavy jaw, and fiery eyes. You were just shorn of your hair! Your neck is paler than the rest of you."

Lucius thought of Father now, with a mixture of anger and grief. "What you say is foolish! If he was here, why did he not become a priest instead of me?"

"And you, never born?" Glyph laughed at the thought. "You have a strong voice. That is well."

Lucius was irritated, and raised his voice more than he wished. "Why do I need a voice in this place? What need is there of such a thing if I am going to spend my life guarding ancient pieces of bark?

Glyph winced with one eye, and the tattoo constricted. "By Egeria! Who told you this is what you would be doing?"

"Everyone at Rome knows it. And I would not do it, unless

I were my father's son, and I had vowed it."

"You are tired and hungry," said Glyph, "and annoyed at your elders, who seem to direct you and yet have no wisdom. Let us take something to eat, and we will talk. Then you will know of what good a voice is, and why we must thank the gods that you have come when you have."

::V::

"*Aquam ventod*," said Glyph, and with his cane gestured to the curtain of water separating the cave from the outside.

A breeze immediately blew up, seeming to come from nowhere, and the water parted for it.

"I am with Kaneesh about getting wet," he said.

Lucius said nothing, just stared at the cane, which Glyph then used to pick his way across the uneven surface of the cave floor.

"Quickly," he said. "The grammar does not last forever."

They passed between the flow of the water, and Lucius continued to stare. The water resumed its natural course with a splash.

Lucius turned back. "*Aquam ventod*," he said.

Nothing happened, except that a bird flitted over them, quick as a thought.

Glyph laughed quietly. "Maybe you'd like to use this," he said. He leaned the cane toward Lucius, and put Lucius' hand on the knob at the top. It was smooth from being handled a long time, and yellowed with age.

Lucius gripped the shaft of the cane, and made an upward flick with it, the way he thought Glyph had done. "*Aquam ventod*," he said.

Nothing.

Glyph said, "It is not so easy as that. Come."

They walked down the stone staircase, Glyph again picking his way, and complaining about being old.

"You do not look so old," Lucius said.

"The apple does not always show the worm," said Glyph.

When they got to the *casula*, Logophilus had already lit a cooking fire and set a low, wide tripod over it. On the tripod he had put a thin, flat disk made of stone, on which he was warming circles of dough. The smell of the bread made Lucius immediately homesick and hungry. It was food he ate every day.

Logophilus put bread before them and began to scramble eggs in a painted bowl. Wild onions went into the mix as well. He stoked the fire up, so that it flared, and poured the egg and onion onto the stone. He took a pinch of salt from another bowl and scattered it over the mixture. It set quickly; Logophilus picked at it with his finger and laid it on another bread. Then he rolled the bread and gave it to Lucius.

"Eat," said Glyph. "The gods are thanked."

Lucius bit down; the egg was creamy and bread soft and yet firm in his mouth. His hunger urging him on, he bit again.

"More salt?" said Glyph, motioning to a small stone bowl on the table.

Lucius shook his head. "It is very good," he said.

"You are polite, young man," said Logophilus, "but we have

salt aplenty."

The meal proceeded in silence as Lucius put his head down and ate. He had rarely been hungrier, nor the food better. After the egg, Logophilus put down curds of goat cheese directly on the flatbread, and it melted and sizzled. Soft leaves of fresh-picked greens went on top of the cheese.

Glyph ate, but slowly, and watched Lucius.

Finally Logophilus sat with them and had his own lunch. He pointed to Lucius and grinned, then rubbed his own belly.

"You have quite an appetite," Glyph said. "It is good that Logo finally gets to eat."

Logophilus threw extra pieces of bread to the dog, which sat with wide eyes, hoping to catch anything that fell from the table.

The afternoon had mellowed. The sun was lower, almost beneath the canopy of the trees. Lucius' belly was full and his eyes heavy-lidded, but his head and heart were full of questions.

"Where do you get the eggs?" he asked. "I do not see any coops."

"They are wild eggs," said Logophilus. "You might better ask where we get the bread." And he motioned out to the clearing, with the vegetable plot and the trees close at hand.

"Oh!" said Lucius. "I hadn't thought of that."

"Now and then we go back to a village nearby, and they are good enough to carry in our grain. The same with our wine and oil. We protect them, and they thank us with provision."

"Protect?"

"Yes. We do not sit here and brood over plane-tree bark, Lucius Junius Brutus," said Glyph. He lifted the cane, made a circle with it. "This land you see-- all of Latium, and Rome itself-- is different from other lands. It has been set apart by the gods to be a root for a great tree that will extend its shade over all lands. The Etruscan *haruspices*, the soothsayers, have already discovered this, which is why they were so interested in conquering Rome and installing their own family of kings. Within the soil of Latium, this land you call home, there is a power that cannot be described."

"From where does the power come?" asked Lucius.

"The land itself. See. I'll show you." Glyph took up his cane, tipped it so that Lucius could see the bony knob, and then pointed underneath. He rotated the cane. Two gold pegs held the knob to the cane.

"Watch," said Glyph. He tapped at a gold peg, then pulled with thumb and forefinger, and it came out. He did the same with the other, and pried the knob off the cane.

Lucius leaned over to look, but Glyph waved him away. He lowered the cane so that three silvery-gray, perfectly spherical stones rolled out of a passage hollowed out of the cane.

"Marbles," said Lucius. "We played with these as boys."

"Not just marbles," said Glyph. "They come from a quarry not far from here. You'll see. Take one in your hand."

Lucius picked one up but almost as quickly put it down. "It's hot!"

"Put a finger on it," said Glyph.

Lucius gingerly did so. He realized it was not hot in temperature, but seemed to vibrate in place.

"Now leave it," said Glyph.

"*Lapis mani ventod*," Glyph said, and held out his palm. *Stone in the hand by the wind*. The marble jumped by itself into Glyph's hand.

"By Hercules," whispered Lucius.

"Long ago, the founders of Rome discovered that these stones, in combination with words of power-- we call it grammar, which is the Greek word for letters-- a trained person could do great feats. Not just moving a curtain of water, or a stone into one's hand, but almost anything you wish."

"Anything?"

"Yes."

"Could you fly to the heavens?"

"Yes."

"Could you go down into the depths of the earth?"

"It would take some doing, but yes."

"Could you stop someone from dying?"

"Yes."

"Could you kill someone?"

"Of course."

"So, this grammar and these stones make you into a god."

"Insofar as we know what god is, yes," said Glyph. "But there is one difference between a god and a user of the grammarstones. Gods do not die. We will."

"So it cannot add a day to one's life?"

"Sometimes," said Glyph. "Depending on how you use them, the grammarstones might make you old before your time."

"So when Father said I would be guarding the lore of the Roman people, did he mean the old writings of Numa? Or the grammarstones?"

"Both," said Glyph. "To become a master of the

grammarstones, to be a *magus magister*, you will need to study what Numa discovered."

"Why did my father not become a *magus magister*? You said you knew him."

"Your father chose not to be. He vowed instead to send a son."

"He was a coward?"

"To the contrary. He was extremely brave. He studied the writings and knew that he would not be able only to guard and protect. He would have used the power to conquer and rule."

"But isn't that the point? He is a good man. He would be a good king."

"It is not so easy. Power changes one. Those who seem noble turn out not to be."

"So we must protect the grammarstones."

"And we must protect the land and the people. Along with the power of Latium, you see, come supernatural things, things that come from gates to other worlds. These are troubling things. You have heard of them. They are called prodigies."

Lucius thought for a moment. "Such as the story of the baby's head in a freshly ploughed furrow, that spoke like an old man?"

"That is one, yes," said Glyph.

"I have heard tell of these prodigies but never knew if they were true."

"That is because you have a mind like the goddess Minerva's. Swift, calculating, practical. Not like that of Mars, which is ruled by anger and fear."

This sounded very sweet to Lucius' ears, and he felt a great excitement coming up in his heart, the opposite of what he had expected. "What is the danger of the prodigies? There is nothing terrible about a baby who speaks, except that it is unusual."

"What you hear about is what happens after the prodigies are weakened and scattered. At the beginning, when they first come from the portal, they are much more powerful. The baby that you heard about is a skilled *magus magister* who has been banished from this world and now and then attempts to come back. He is one of our most troubling foes. When he is weak, he turns up as a prodigy, a harmless thing that frightens children, and gives soothsayers something from which to predict the future."

Lucius hit on something, and spoke as he considered it. "You mean that we-- that the *magus magister*-- that there is a battle--"

"Yes, we use the grammarstones to attack and defend."

"So. I am to be a warrior. I really am."

"Yes," said Glyph. "When you swam the Tiber, it was a true impulse-- a true gift of your genius, for you to stand and protect your nation, Rome. You simply will not do it with a sword and a spear. You will do it with a cane, your mind, and the grammarstones."

"You know I swam the Tiber?"

"We have been waiting for you, Lucius Junius called Brutus," said Glyph. "We have been preparing for a long time."

::VI::

Lucius had never had trouble sleeping, and that night, despite all that he heard from Glyph and Logophilus, when he put his had down on the straw-filled mattress laid out for him on the floor of Logophilus' hut, he was asleep in no time.

But he was awake again, deep in the night, perhaps wakened by Logophilus' resonant snoring, perhaps by a need to relieve himself. He ducked out of the hut and went to the shed set apart on a slope in the woods. The stars were a creamy blaze; no moon made them all the brighter, and there would be no rain or clouds to obscure them for many a month.

Glyph was sleeping in the cave, with the dog, or so he said, but as Lucius walked back from the shed, the dog silently appeared, panting, her feet making no sound on the soft earth under the eaves of the laurel tree.

"You seem to be everywhere, I think, Kaneesh," said Lucius. He ventured out from the tree, and something caught his eye across the clearing with its garden and low wall.

Kaneesh pricked up her ears and was gone in a moment, hopping lightly over the wall without disturbing the loose pieces of shingle topping it.

Lucius leaned over the wall and narrowed his eyes. He saw three slim heads in the distance, with long snouts and shying ears: deer, come to plunder the plants that were much sweeter than the mallow and sow thistle growing wild.

They popped up on to the stone wall, skinny-legged, skittish creatures, and were about to lean down over into the vegetable rows, when there came two quick barks, followed by Kaneesh herself on the wall, her tail whirling.

The deer turned and ran, and the only evidence of their having been there was the sound of them crashing through bushes at the edge of the clearing.

A few moments later, Kaneesh was back, panting, her feet making no sound on the soft ground.

"You protect the land and the people, too," said Lucius, giving the dog a companionable scratch behind the ears. "Hey!"

Lucius took his hand away from the dog's head as if he'd been bitten. The soft fur around the ears had suddenly gone rigid.

Again, Kaneesh hopped onto the wall and then over between rows of beets and carrots. Her ears were back and tail up.

Lucius heard something like grumbling coming from the garden. *Is that the dog growling?* he thought at first, but the noise sounded human. He followed Kaneesh, picking his way down the rows of vegetables.

As they got closer, the noise began more and more to

sound like a person speaking in an unknown tongue. It sounded like "waw, waw, waw" to Lucius.

Finally, in an unplanted area of the patch, they came upon what looked like a pale, silver cabbage. As they came closer, Lucius saw that it was a human head, and that it was moving its mouth and speaking. It had no hair, tiny ears, and glowed like the moon. Its face was turned from them, but its jaws were working as it kept saying its "waw, waw, waw."

Kaneesh circled it, and Lucius followed. The face was of a baby, as if in pain, needing to be fed, its stomach upset. The eyes were screwed tightly shut, the mouth working back and forth. For the first time, Lucius heard words instead of sounds. The baby was speaking Latin and saying, *canem bonum, canem bonum-- good dog, good dog.*

Lucius didn't know what to do. It was a strange thing to see late at night under a sky with no moon, but it didn't seem to be threatening or even aware that the dog and boy were there.

Kaneesh sat a safe distance away, ears pricked. She wasn't taking any chances. But Lucius crept forward. He was seeing the talking baby prodigy he had heard about. What if it had some wisdom to tell Lucius? Or perhaps it would have a message to relay to Glyph. There seemed to be nothing to fear.

He knelt in front of the baby head as it continued to mouth its canem bonum chant, and slowly extended his hand toward it. Should he touch it?

The dog growled, then whined. As Lucius' outstretched fingers came closer, they began to feel a heat, and a tingling, like that from the marble that Glyph had allowed him to touch.

Then, without warning, the baby opened its eyes and mouth wide and stopped grumbling. Lucius looked down into the depths of the throat, blue-green, wet with saliva, with palpitating tonsils, and saw embedded in the back of the throat and the tonsils rows and rows of spheres, about the size of grammarstones.

Then the baby screamed. It sounded like the scream of someone in the worst pain imaginable.

Lucius fell back in a somersault and landed with his face in the dirt. He got up and ran. He had never run so fast. He felt as if the head was chasing him; the screaming echoed through his entire body, and pierced like knives. He was out of the garden in no time. He rushed into Logophilus' hut, leaned over his cot, and shook him. He could not speak. The hair on the nape of his neck was straight up; he was sweating and ice cold at the same time. As if in a dream, he couldn't speak. He couldn't feel his lips or tongue, but his teeth smarted.

"Unngh, unngh, unngh," was all he could get out.

Logophilus sat up. "What is it? Did you dream?"

"Waw, waw, waw," said Lucius, and pointed.

"Did you see something? What is it, child?"

"*Ganem ponum*," said Lucius, and shuddered.

Glyph appeared at the threshold. "I heard a scream."

Logophilus held Lucius by the arms and turned him to Glyph.

Glyph knelt down, took him by the chin, and said, "*Spes sanguinem iuvenis spiritod*," *Hope into the blood of the boy*, by breath. Then he drew air into his cheeks and blew it gently at him.

Lucius fell to the ground, and began to sob. Feeling came back into his mouth; his limbs loosened.

"What did you see?" Glyph said.

"*Canem... bonum...*" said Lucius, his whole body heaving

with sobs.

"*Canem bonum*?" said Glyph. *Good dog.*

"He is seeking Egeria," said Logophilus.

"I think so," said Glyph. "Let us go see."

They pulled Lucius up, who said *no, no, no.*

"He cannot hurt you," said Glyph. "Only scare you."

"Let's go," said Logophilus, supporting Lucius with a long arm under Lucius' opposite arm.

"No, please," said Lucius, wiping his face.

"It will be much worse soon," said Glyph. "Fear is not the worst thing."

"Worst?" sobbed Lucius.

Glyph and Logophilus managed, between the two of them, to get Lucius walking, and as he walked, he finally pushed them away, ashamed and angry that he had bawled like a child. Nevertheless, he let Glyph go first, and kept Logophilus at his side, who held him by the shoulder.

When they got to the field where the head lay, Kaneesh joined them, and took up a spot in the same place she had sat before.

Lucius thought, *I am foolish! It does not even have arms or legs!* Nevertheless, he couldn't bring himself to look straight at it, and he put his hands to his ears, should it scream again.

The thing was grumbling again, *canem bonum canem bonum*, its eyes shut and mouth working.

Glyph flipped his cane into the air and caught it by the skinny end, as if he was going to use it like a club against the head. But then, with a flick of the wrist, he brought it down and back.

"*Lapis prodigium*," he said, *the stone against the prodigy*, and flicked the cane forward again. There was the sound of a grammarstone clicking in the hollow chamber of the knob. Then he waved the cane forward, and with another flick of the wrist, a hinge on the knob loosed itself, and a marble came flying out on a low line.

The baby opened its mouth. The marble flew into it. And the baby disappeared.

"Gone," said Logophilus. "And he won a grammarstone for his troubles."

Kaneesh whined, and walked around the area where the head had been, sniffing.

"Was that the *magus magister*?" Lucius finally whispered.

"The very one," said Glyph. "He paid you a visit. Only I think we should call him the horrible master: *malus magister*."

"But you said he couldn't hurt me. Only scare me."

"In this form. But he, or his servants, will be back when the time is right, when they have gathered their strength."

"There were marbles in his throat."

"Not enough, for now. But soon he will have more."

"Why did you give him one?"

"To make him go away, of course." He did not explain further.

Lucius groaned and threw up his hands. "I am a coward. I blubbered like a baby."

"On the contrary," said Logophilus. "You did well."

"I would not come back to see a mere baby head," said Lucius. "You had to carry me, Logo."

"I did not make your legs work. That was your doing."

"Kaneesh was not afraid. A dog!"

"You did better than your father," Glyph put in.

41

"I did?" Lucius relaxed at this, stood up straighter, rotated his shoulders.

"After his first prodigy, he curled into a ball and wouldn't move from morning to night," Glyph said, working the hinge on the cane knob.

Lucius rubbed his eyes. The image of the head was still there, and the feeling of being surrounded by knives. He could hardly stand, but he was standing.

"A good voice, a stout heart, and shame," Glyph said. "All these things are needful for a priest of Numa Pompilius."

Logophilus bowed to Lucius. "Three needful things."

A grudging smile creased Lucius' cheek.

"Let us have breakfast," Glyph said. "The sun will be up soon, and fighting prodigies gives me a powerful appetite.

To his surprise, Lucius felt hungry, too. His stomach was all jumbled and jangled from the scream, but the emptiness of his belly gnawed at him, and the weakness in his limbs, he knew, would be banished by warm flatbread in his stomach.

At the sound of breakfast, Kaneesh barked.

"You are always hungry, dog," said Logophilus.

"It is well," said Glyph. "She has done her work tonight, too."

::VII::

The sun rose as they ate, flatbread with salt sprinkled over, and after a cup of wine mixed with water and a conversation about vegetables, deer, seasons of planting, and what amount of salt makes bread tastes best, Glyph and Lucius, feeling much more settled, left Logophilus and Kaneesh to tend the garden, and they set out for the grammarstone quarry.

"This is also what you are protecting," said Glyph, pointing upwards toward the quarry as they walked past the curtain of water. "The prodigies must be kept from escaping their world, but equally, the quarry cannot fall into the hands of those from outside who will use it for ill."

They walked up more stairs, which ended at the summit of an outcrop of rock that baked in the early-morning sun. The day would be hot; no clouds tempered the light of the sun as it flew like a grammarstone through the sky.

In the distance, a thin blue line signaled the sea, and Rome was somewhere under the ribbons of smoke from cooking fires trailing like fillets from some heavenly bull's horns.

Glyph leaned on the cane for support. "We are not so far from Rome, as you can see," he said, between huffs and puffs.

"Yet I walked all day between here and there," said Lucius, feeling the ache in his legs still.

They made their way across the rocky knob and down again, this time by a dirt path and in the shade of wild olive trees. Tawny rye grass with nodding grain ears grew up on the edges of their canopies. Ahead of them a rock wall came into view, within a hollow cut into the hillside. Two olive trees stood on either side of the path as it flattened and led into the recess, long by fifty paces and wide by forty.

The rock wall itself was steep and much higher than the highest rooftree in Rome, and grayish in color, like that of the cave and outcrop, with tiny veins of silver. As they came closer, Lucius saw that the rock was pockmarked with tiny holes in some places, and discolored, darker gray, and even brown.

Glyph's voice echoed from the wall as he spoke, making his words seem somehow more than human. "This is one of the sources of Latium's power. There are many gates to the other world near here, caves, places from which hot water gushes."

"Are we in danger here?" asked Lucius.

"We must go further in to find the sources of the other world," said Glyph. "But soon enough, the prodigies will find us. Do not fear, Lucius. This place is for practice." He flipped up the cane as he done earlier that day, clicked a grammarstone into the chamber, and said, "*Lapis lapidem ignid.*" *Stone against stone with fire.*

Another flick of the wrist, and the chambered stone flew out and covered the distance between them and the wall in no time. There was a loud bang, and the stone exploded into a fireball. The sound of the explosion echoed in the quarry, and a puff of smoke slowly migrated upwards and dissipated.

Lucius jumped, then whispered, "By Hercules."

Glyph said, "A useful grammar, is it not? Do you want to try?"

Lucius nodded, still staring at the place in the wall where the grammarstone had hit and imprinted the stone with a little seal of black smoke.

"No grammar. Just try to work the cane."

It took some doing even to get a grammarstone chambered, but the wrist action was not unlike that of the wooden short swords with which he had bouted Arruns and other boys his age.

"Now let it fly," said Glyph.

"It won't," said Lucius, after trying several times. His wrist began to smart. "The hinge is broken."

"It is not broken," said Glyph. He took the cane from Lucius, and whirled it in a half-circle. A grammarstone flew out and rattled against the wall.

"Now I have to re-chamber," said Lucius, frowning. He shook his hand and flexed his fingers several times before taking the cane back from Glyph.

"Patience," said Glyph. "You cannot be a *magus magister* all at once."

It took a long time to get a stone into the knob again, but Glyph would not help him. Lucius wanted to throw the cane against the wall, and almost did. The sweat on his hand left the cane slippery in his grip, and as he in his frustration tried a violent wrist-flick, the cane flew out of his hands and went end-over-end into the air.

"It'll break!" shouted Lucius.

"*Cornu mani ventod*," said Glyph, *horn in the hand by the wind*, and a little puff of air came up, made Lucius' tunic whip, and caught the cane in mid-air. The cane stopped twirling, and instead flipped once and landed in Glyph's hand.

"Never fear," said Glyph. "I think that is all for one day. It is a good first day."

"But I didn't make the grammarstone fly from the cane," said Lucius. "And we took no time at all."

"Time is like salt for us," said Glyph. "There is plenty, and you will be here every day practicing, when you are not studying grammar. And we should not snap the tendons in your wrist the first day, eh?"

Lucius felt his wrist with his other hand. It was like he'd been through a whole day of sword fighting.

Glyph leaned on the cane again, as if it were just a cane, and waited for Lucius to lead the way back the *casula*. But Lucius walked up to the rock wall and touched the place where the stone had exploded. Just like the marbles and the head, the rock sent off some kind of vibration that made Lucius' fingers tingle. He wanted to rub the surface of the rock, but the tingling went into his arm, and finally made his ear hurt.

Lucius turned and shook his arm out. Glyph stood apart, saying nothing, neither smiling nor frowning. Lucius kicked at a loose stone and set it skittering. His ears still hurt, and he still felt the hum of the rock.

Then, without knowing exactly why, he said, "*Lapis lapidem ventod.*" *Stone against stone with wind.* The loose piece he had kicked flew up and came straight for him. He had only a moment to duck before the stone slammed into the wall and smashed into a thousand pieces.

Glyph called, "You are stubborn, Lucius Junius Brutus. Come now. Truly, it is over for today."

Lucius coughed and waved away the cloud of stone-dust the explosion had made. He brushed dust from his hair and shoulders. Dust in his nose smelled burnt.

Nevertheless, he ran to Glyph and smiled. "I have perfected my grammar," he said.

"And almost dashed your brains out," said Glyph. "Never do that again. Never make grammar unless I give you leave. You do not know what could happen."

Lucius examined Glyph's expression. No anger there, and his tone was neutral as well. "But it means, perhaps, that I do not have to study so much, and I can spend more time here with the cane?"

"On the contrary," said Glyph. "Your nearness to the wall caused your grammar to have power. It is the strength of the grammarstone that made that grammar perfect, not the words themselves."

"I don't understand," said Lucius. "When they are just words, simple words I know, what is there to learn?"

"Exactly the reason we are going now away from here," said Glyph. "The second part of the day begins as soon as you consent to stop throwing stones at your own head."

Lucius smiled sheepishly, but Glyph would not smile back at him.

They walked back out of the quarry, and when they got to the rocky outcrop the strengthening sun fell on Lucius' wrist and relieved the pain some. Down the stairs again and through the curtain of water, "*aquam ventod*," they picked their way along the uneven cave floor and finally went through the threshold to Glyph's inner chamber.

The room was lit by oil lamps, many of them, made from metal or pottery, some with designs, others without. Some were lit, others were not; there was the sour smell of olive oil, and the ceiling was black with oil smoke.

The chamber held a small bed, a large table for writing, and a cabinet of six shelves, filled with skin scrolls. On the table there was plane tree bark, many sheets of it, and a stylus and inkpot for writing on the bark.

"Is this where the writings of Numa are kept?" asked Lucius.

"Yes and no," said Glyph, and would say no more about it. Instead, he took out a scroll from the cabinet, swept away the sheets of plane bark to the side of the table, and unrolled the scroll.

The scroll was written on from end to end, in signs that Lucius did not understand. He knew that Etruscan could be written down, and that Etruscan priests would write out prayers and contracts and read them aloud, but Lucius had rarely seen Latin written in letters. The signs he had made with Demetria were based on the Greek letters she had learned by looking at notations her father had made concerning his wool business.

"This sign will say *ara*," Demetria had said, scratching a square on bark with her fingernail. "And this one--" she made a circle, and cut a line through it horizontally-- "will say *na*. *Ara-na*. *Vale*. Farewell."

"These signs are all Latin," said Glyph. "They are based on

the Etruscan alphabet, which comes from the Greek alphabet. When you know the signs, you can make words, and then grammar."

Lucius frowned. "But what use is the writing? Cannot we simply remember, and speak?"

"Anyone with access to grammarstones can learn to make grammar with practice. Logo has learned a few things just by observing me. But a priest of Numa has more discipline than that. The writing is a kind of practice and an aid to memory. When you are in battle with a prodigy, you will not remember your grammar, unless you have studied it. Fear gets in the way, and they have power to distract your mind itself. When you study writing enough, it is emblazoned on your mind's eye. You see it, and you know it, regardless of what is happening around you."

Glyph held the scroll open in the middle, where the writing was divided into seven rows and five columns, and there were groups of signs in each of the intersections of the rows and columns.

"These are the Thirty-Five," said Glyph. "This is what you must study."

"I can make nothing of it," said Lucius.

"You will. Here--" and he traced his finger down the edge of the seven rows--"are the *possibilities*, what you can do with grammar." Then he pulled his finger over the top of the columns. "These are the *kinds*, the groups of words you use to make grammar."

"And in the middle? These?" Lucius pointed to the grid of thirty-five jumbles of signs enclosed by the possibilities and kinds, making a pattern like woven fabric.

"These are words, examples of words you can use," Glyph said. "This one is *aqua*, water. This one is *ventus*, air. *Lapis*, stone, is the third, *manus*, hand, the fourth, and the last one is *spes*, hope."

"You used that one, *spes*, on me."

"To encourage you when you were afraid, yes. And these words are quite useful, which is why they are written as examples. But there are many others, as many as you can think of."

Lucius saw that the signs of each of the kinds were the same for their first letters, but changed somewhat in their endings. This made sense, because in Latin, depending on what you wanted to say, you often changed the ending of a word. So that if you wanted someone to give you water, you would not say *aqua*, but *aquam*. But if you wanted to say that the water was good, you would say *aqua*. He told this to Glyph, who nodded.

"Yes," he said. "All the different possibilities of *aqua* are here, and you will learn them."

"Can you tell them to me now?"

"Quickly." He pointed to the first possibility. "This is the Caller. It is what you use when you want something that is not there to appear."

"By Hercules. Is it so?"

"Of course. Now, listen." He took his finger down one row. "This one is the Namer. You use it when you want something, like water, to do a task for you.

"This one is the Striker. You use it when you want something to be attacked, changed, or affected in some way.

"This is the Bestower. You use this to tell the Namer for whom or what something is being done.

"This is the Builder. You use this to tell the Namer how or with what tool something should be done.

"This is the Owner. You use it to tell the Namer to whom it or something else belongs.

"Finally, this is the Placer. You use it to tell the namer where something is or should be."

When he had finished, and spoken all the possibilities of *aqua*, Lucius said, "I know all these possibilities, and speak many of them every day. It is the Latin language."

"Correct," said Glyph. "But spoken with the power of the grammarstones, and in the proper order, with the proper movements of cane, or hand, or even mind, it is a strength against which nothing in the world except the gods can stand."

"By Hercules! How can it be?" said Lucius.

"It is a mystery none of us understand fully. But once you spoke the words *aquam ventod*, to try to change the course of the waterfall. Nothing happened. Then, in the quarry, with the living stone at your back, you said *lapis lapidem ventod*, and you almost died on the spot. This is how we know the grammar is perfect. These are the Thirty-Five."

This is what the table looked like:

	First	Second	Third	Fourth	Fifth
Summoner	o terra	o vente	o lapis	o manus	o spes
Namer	terra	ventus	lapis	manus	spes
Striker	terram	ventom	lapidem	manum	spem
Bestower	terrae	vento	lapidei	manui	spei
Builder	terrad	ventod	lapidid	manud	sped
Owner	terrais	venti	lapidis	manuos	speis
Placer	terrai	ventei	lapidi	mani	spi

"Now we must be done with work for the day," said Glyph.

"You have already learned much. There is nothing more you can do."

"But I don't feel tired, Glyph. I can continue working."

"Tomorrow, Lucius."

Lucius nodded, and gazed at the Thirty-Five, his eyes shining. "If only Demetria could see this," he whispered to himself.

And Glyph smiled.

::VIII::

That evening, Logophilus told Lucius not to go walking the garden by himself at night.

"You do not know what will appear," said Logo.

Lucius nodded vigorously and assured the old man that he would stay close to home. He fell asleep immediately and woke after the sun rose.

Logo was not in the *casula*, and neither was Kaneesh. Logo had left the cook fire warm with good, orange embers, and had left a pot of barley porridge on a tripod. Lucius poked the embers to life and put a couple more sticks on it to warm the porridge, then ladled it out into a bowl, grateful for the food that warmed his belly.

While Lucius was eating, Glyph arrived from the cave.

"Where is Logo?" said Lucius, as he wiped the last of his porridge with scraps of flatbread left on the cooking disc.

"And greetings to you, too, young man," said Glyph. "*Salve.*"

"I'm sorry. *Salve*, Glyph."

53

"He headed for the village before the sun rose," said Glyph. He took a bowl, scooped out some porridge for himself, and salted it. "He was on the hunt for a metal cooking spoon. And he will bring news."

"Of what?"

"Of prodigies, if there are any. This is where they first appear. If they come to Rome, then something has gone wrong with us."

Logophilus and Kaneesh returned around midday, after Lucius and Glyph had had a lesson in detecting and writing the signs of the Roman alphabet.

"Someone claims to have seen a shower of blood in the distance last night," said Logo.

"There has not been a cloud since I came here," said Lucius.

"Sometimes what a peasant sees is not red rain, but the distant smoke of cooking fires caught in the sunset," said Glyph.

"They gave me this," said Logo. It was a cutting of grapevine stained with a thick, rust-red liquid. "They said they lost a whole field to it, grapes that had been yielding well for a decade."

Kaneesh sniffed the vine, and growled.

"Not just blood, but poison," said Glyph. "We may be looking for a snake. And we need to leave right away."

"Am I going?" said Lucius.

"Of course," said Glyph.

They hurried up the stairs, past the rock outcrop, and into the quarry. Glyph leaned on the cane, but walked surprisingly fast. When they got to the wall itself, Glyph pointed upwards, and said, "There is a hidden portal up there, about halfway up. I need you to climb and see what you find."

"Climb?"

"The portal is behind the face of the wall. There is a little ledge, and if you look around the face, there will be a hole."

Lucius looked up. The quick pace of the walk had made him sweat but now fear added to it. An icy drop of moisture trickled down his side from under his arm.

"I don't know if--"

"Never fear."

"It's not fear," said Lucius, although he knew it was. "I don't know what to do if--"

"I am with you," said Glyph. "If something comes from the portal, I will deal with it."

"Deal with it?"

"If you can see the prodigy first, before it attacks, then we will know what it is. We will have an advantage."

Lucius shook his head, and shuddered, but he turned to the wall. He looked back at Glyph again, who pointed upwards. Lucius shed his sandals and tried the rock; he had done a little climbing on a cliff in Rome called the Tarpeian Rock.

He easily found handholds and rests for his feet, and soon he was high above Glyph, who looked up at him and called out gentle encouragement.

Glyph's ledge was not much bigger than a footrest, but standing on it, Lucius didn't have to hold on so tight with his hands above him. Instead, he inched his way to the left with his hands at about hip height.

Sure enough, as he pivoted around an outcrop of rock, the ledge opened up almost into a split wide enough for a path. No more than a few paces away, a gap in the rock, at knee level, nearly square, led into darkness.

"I found it," Lucius said, turning briefly to Glyph to say it.

"Good work," said Glyph. "Now go toward it."

"I will not be able to see in the dark."

"*Lucs mani iuvenis minima*," said Glyph, *light on the hand of the youth... very small*, and let fly a grammarstone from the cane. A little glowing orb flickered in front of Lucius and settled on a knuckle of his hand just above his ring finger. It tickled just like a regular grammarstone would.

Lucius thanked Glyph, and got down on his hands and knees to fit into the gap in the rock, which spanned somewhat less than the distance from Lucius' nose to his extended forefinger.

Lucius took the glowing stone in his hand, and held it in his closed palm, until he was used to the tickle and felt it more as a vibration in his funny bone. He said, "*lapis antrei*," *the stone in the cave*, and opened his palm.

Nothing happened.

Lucius licked sweat from his lip, wiped it from his brow. The opening was still dark. Maybe there was nothing in there.

He inched forward and peered in, the grammarstone still in his hand. The sunlight tricked him: as long as he was in it, his eyes would see blackness. But if he stuck his head in, by the light of the grammarstone, his eyes would adjust and perhaps see the prodigy that had caused the blood rain.

Glyph said, "Are you all right? Do you need more light?"

"All right. No more light, not yet."

Lucius' knees began to ache on the bare stone. No more delay; he had to either go in, or take the coward's path, and back out.

I am a priest, and I am a warrior, he told himself.

Holding the grammarstone out in front of him with his elbow on the rock, he crawled forward. The stone lit up the threshold of the portal, gray stone. Lucius went forward still more. His head was almost inside. The light lit up the sides of the cave, gray stone.

Lucius stopped when his head and shoulders were inside. He realized he could crawl in if he wanted to.

Once again, he said, "*lapis antrei.*"

This time the grammarstone buzzed in his hand, like an insect, but did not move out of it. It only illuminated cave walls to the left and right. The inside was still pitch black.

Lucius considered what he could do. He could ask the grammarstone to strike the cave: *lapis antrom*, but he didn't know what that would do.

Or he could just throw the stone and hope that it stopped somewhere where its light would be visible.

Lucius looked back out the hole, was blinded for a second by the sunlight. He could go out again and ask Glyph's advice. But that seemed to him a way to waste much time.

Once more, he held the grammarstone in his clenched palm, let the vibrations of the stone flow up through his arm, closed his eyes tightly, and then opened his palm again.

"*Lapis antrei.*" *The stone in the cave.*

He didn't know exactly what happened next. He felt as if he might have opened his palm so quickly and with such a jerk that the grammarstone jumped out of it. Or maybe the stone left because of the grammar.

In any case, it went flying up and into the cave, and it lit up a long passage of stone.

It also lit up a snake: huge, scaly, with open jaws, a flickering tongue, and twin fangs.

Lucius jerked back, hit his head on the cave ceiling, and fell forward. The cave seemed to tilt. With a scrabble of stones, he began to slide forward, his big toes scraping against dust and gravel.

"Glyph!" Lucius yelled, before he began really to fall into the cave, the walls of which seemed to widen out as he did so. He thrashed his arms and legs, and just before he was about to fall into the jaws of the snake, he screamed, "*lapis serpentem!*" *The stone against the snake.*

There was a bang, the light went out, and Lucius' jaw slammed violently into hard soil mixed with rock. Dirt shucked up between his teeth and into his mouth. His body followed, and for a second his head rang and his limbs would not respond.

"By Hercules!" Lucius groaned, spitting dirt. He managed to turn over, and when he did, he saw the light from the opening to the cave, far above him. Otherwise it was dark.

The good news was that there was no snake. The grammarstone had taken care of that. Lucius rejoiced that he had really perfected at least one grammar. Maybe one that saved his life.

The question was, how to get out?

He knelt, then stood. He could not see the walls of the cave, but by feeling with his hands and using the hole of the cave as a guide, he found a wall.

"Back up by climbing," Lucius said to himself. "It's not far."

He found footrests and handholds, as he had on the

outside, and had made good progress when he heard something below him.

It was a hissing.

Another snake? thought Lucius. *The same one?* He held tightly to the rock wall, unable to climb further. His mind washed over with fear; he could not think about feeling for the next handhold. But the opening to the cave was not far. If only...

The hissing came again, and was closer. *Can it climb?* thought Lucius. *Some snakes can climb trees. Or maybe it's so big it will just pluck me from this wall.* He hated that he couldn't see it. He hated that he hadn't a grammarstone to help him.

And where in the name of all the gods was Glyph?

Thinking of Glyph gave him an idea. Maybe he did have a grammarstone. After all, they came from this very quarry. The cliff itself was full of power.

Lucius worried free a chunk of rock. It did not vibrate like the spherical, worked stone had. But Lucius felt a vibration.

The hissing came even closer, and now Lucius smelled something, something foul, like rotten meat and dirty sweat mixed together, and his stomach fell out from under him. He wanted to hold his nose, but that would mean losing his grip on the face of the wall.

SSSSSSSSSST.

Something licked at Lucius' feet. He screamed, and started to say *lapis serpentem* again, but couldn't get the words out. Instead, he threw the rock as hard as he could. He almost lost hold as he threw; one foot dangled free from the wall. But he was able to get a hold again with his throwing hand, and his foot clamped back to its rest.

The rock hit something-- there was a thump-- and bounced

up. As it did, it glowed, and illuminated the cave for a second. A huge snake, much bigger than the first, had been slithering toward him and could almost touch the soles of his sandals. The snake was also writhing, as a trickle of blood was trailing into its eye. The rock had split its scales open.

Lucius held tightly to the cliff, concentrating only on keeping a hold. Could he kick the snake back down if it came up again?

He didn't want to take that chance. Panting hard, he cast about in his head for a grammar that might do something, anything.

And something inside him, his genius perhaps, gave him this:

"*Iuvens terrai ventod.*" *The young man on the ground by the wind.*

A whirlwind tore Lucius from the rock. He hurtled upwards. Lucius closed his eyes and shielded his head in his hands. Don't hit the wall as I come out, he screamed to himself.

He did hit the wall, glancing off it, and scraped all four of his knuckles on both hands. Then he flew out and into the sunlight, and as he somersaulted up, his limbs windmilled in thin air.

"Glyph, Help meeeeeeeee!" he screamed.

Lucius saw sky, earth, sky, earth, and then Glyph.

Another wind took Lucius as he heard Glyph say, "*iuvens terrai ventod incolums.*" *The young man on the ground by the wind... unharmed.* Lucius stopped turning, and the wind from Glyph spread Lucius on his back, buoying him up like the River Tiber, and gently depositing him on the ground again in front of Glyph.

Lucius looked up at his mentor through sweat pouring down over his eyes.

"Well, then. Did you see anything?" Glyph asked.

::IX::

Lucius got up, dusted himself off, inspected his arms and legs. His clothes were muddy, his whole body covered in sweat, but everything seemed to be in its right place.

Glyph inspected him, too. "You look as if you've been dipped in a swamp," he said. "And you are glowing like a grammarstone."

"I thought you said you would be my ally," Lucius said.

"And I was. As far as you'd let me be."

"Let?"

"You clearly made a decision to go inside the cave without my help."

"Well, there wasn't room for two," said Lucius.

Glyph motioned to the path out of the quarry. "Let's get you cleaned up. What happened to the grammarstone?"

Lucius told him as they walked. The shade in the quarry, combined with the wetness of his body, made him feel almost cold. When they came out to the rocky knob, the sun hit him full and he went gooseflesh. He felt dead tired all of a sudden, and paused in the telling of his story.

"Being a warrior is hard work, is it not?" said Glyph. "We will have to deal with this snake, but it is good that you delayed it from exiting the portal. It would have been much more dangerous otherwise."

"Will it not come out while we are gone?"

"It will nurse its wound. You made a good throw, I think. Never fear. If it leaves the portal, I will find and stop it. I have much practice with this sort of thing."

They stopped at the curtain of water so that Lucius could rinse off. Glyph fetched clothes from his cave, and he went down to the *casula* and let Lucius dry off and change in peace.

Before he went, he cocked his head at Lucius and said, "You know, you didn't have to go inside the cave. You could have just dropped the stone and let it illuminate the inside. There was no need to try to perfect a grammar."

"I wanted to," said Lucius. Glyph's words puzzled and annoyed him. He thought he would be prouder of what Lucius had done.

For a moment, the only sound was the curtain of water splashing on the stones. Glyph stared at Lucius for a moment, as if he were about to say something, but then turned and went down the stone stairs, his cane clicking as he went.

Lucius took his time underneath the cold but refreshing water, rinsed out his clothes and laid them to dry, and put on the ones Glyph had given him. The leggings and tunic were too big for him, but manageable. They were made of fine linen and felt new or as if they had not been worn for a long time.

While he did all this, he kept thinking two thoughts that battled and would not surrender to the other: *Glyph would not help me* and *I would not let Glyph help me.*

He walked down and found Logo, Kaneesh, and Glyph at the cookfire. Logo had spitted and was grilling sausages he had obtained in the village. The savory smell reminded Lucius he was ravenous.

"After the meal, we spend the rest of the day in letters," said Glyph. "If you are going to try grammar, you should at least know some."

"The master told me you perfected a grammar inside the portal of the prodigies," Logo said. "I congratulate you." He gave him a broad smile and a pat on the back. "You are a quick study, Lucius Junius Brutus." He smiled as he lifted out a sausage dripping with fat from its spit, holding it out to Lucius.

"Thank you," said Lucius. "When I--"

"There is no need to congratulate nor to recount stories, Logo," said Glyph. "And you, Lucius. You are overconfident. You will hurt yourself. It is not something to play at."

"Yes, master," said Logo, eyeing Lucius ruefully.

"Yes, Glyph," said Lucius. He held the spit with the sausage, wondering if he should eat.

"There will be time for stories. Now is time for study."

They thanked the gods, ate sausage and flatbread, and sipped wine mixed with spring water. Lucius felt revived, enough to go back to the quarry and finish off the snake if he had to.

Instead they went to Glyph's cave, and Glyph rolled out another scroll, a different one, with a different chart. There were still the seven possibilities, but now there were only three kinds, and the words were different.

"These words are called companions. They join hands with

the words of the Thirty-Five, and shape what they are and do."

From his study yesterday, Lucius could make out some of the letters with which the companions were written. Here was a "P," here an "A," but he did not know all of them.

"Do you remember when I sent you the grammarstone? I named *lucs*, light, and asked that it rest on your hand, *mani*. But then there was another namer at the end, a companion for the first namer."

"*Minima.* Very small."

"Yes. That described what the light would be, rather than great, blinding, blood-red, pale, what have you."

Lucius stared down at the clusters of letters. Here was an "R," which was like a "P," but they had different sounds.

"Later, when you were spinning in the air above me and about to dash out your brains on the quarry floor, I named you, the youth, *iuvens*, and asked that you be put down by the wind, *ventod*, but, again, I spoke another namer at the end, another companion."

"*Incolums.* Unharmed."

"Which is exactly what you forgot to say when you perfected your grammar about the wind taking you back to the ground."

"I didn't know I *could* say that," Lucius grumbled.

"Well, of course. That is why we study." Glyph turned to the chart. "There are three kinds of companion: two can be both the first and second kind, and one can only be the third kind."

He showed Lucius the word *parva*, *small*, written in the first two columns. This was the one with the P-A-R in it. The endings of *parva* were exactly like the endings of the first two kinds of the thirty-five-- Glyph proved it by bringing out the scroll with the Thirty-Five and comparing the signs. He then showed Lucius the third kind, with the word *forts*, *brave* or *strong*. Again, the endings of that word were the same as the endings of the third kind in the Thirty-Five.

This is how it looked on the companion chart:

	First	Second	Third
Summoner	o parva	o parve	o forts
Namer	parva	parvus	forts
Striker	parvam	parvom	fortem
Bestower	parvae	parvo	fortei
Builder	parvad	parvod	fortid
Owner	parvais	parvi	fortis
Locator	parvai	parvei	forti

"So," Lucius said, "if I wanted to summon a drop of water, small water, would I say, *o parva o aqua*?"

"No," said Glyph. He made a flick of his cane. "*O parva aqua* is sufficient." And a little teardrop of water fell from the end of the cane.

"And *o magna aqua*? To summon great water? Can I do that?"

"I would not try it without knowing more grammar. Great water will drown you, I think, even if you perfect the grammar."

"And if I wanted to summon strong water, would it be *o forta aqua*?"

"No, indeed. It would be *o forts aqua*. The companion of the third kind cannot change its ending as can the companion of the first two kinds."

"And what about the companions of the fourth and fifth

kind? Where are they?"

"There are no such companions. You may use those of the first, second, and third if you need to. For the fourth and fifth kinds do not like to have companions; they are like the mountain cat that hunts alone."

"It is not so difficult," said Lucius, hoping not to sound-- what was it that Glyph had said?-- overconfident. "I have used companions in Latin all the time, to tell others what I want or what I think something is. I remember once when I traveled with my father to Ostia as a very young child, I saw the sea for the first time. *Quam aqua est magna*! I cried. *The water is so big*."

"What did he say?"

"I remember exactly. It is one of the first things I ever remember him telling me. He said, *you must not say* aqua *but* mare."

"And what did you say?"

I said, *mare est magna, o pater*! *The sea is big, Papa*!"

"Your father must have corrected you and said we must say *mare est magnom*."

"That is exactly what he said. How he and my mother laughed about it when we returned home."

"That is a difficult one to remember, for that grammar is a wild one, as is the sea." Glyph tapped the scroll thoughtfully, and was about to say something else, but did not.

Lucius said, "Of course it was a difficult grammar when I was a young child. But I am a man, now."

"You are a young priest now. And when you are in a battle with a prodigy, you must know your possibilities, kinds, and companions as quickly as if you were speaking at the dinner table at your home. More quickly than if you were asking for some favor from the king. And for that, you must study."

Glyph motioned to the chair in front of the writing table. A great pile of bark sat on the right, and the stylus and inkpot on the left. "I want you to copy the signs that you see on this scroll. You have an excellent memory and are a great speaker of Latin. But to study, you must learn how to read. And to read, you must know how to write, for your hand will tell you what the signs say."

"I will," said Lucius, remembering Demetria and their play language. Soon she would be old enough to marry. He thought of her as a mother, with children about her, weaving all the time in her husband's house, and teaching her nieces to weave, as her aunt had done for her.

"Well?" said Glyph.

"What?" Lucius looked up.

"There shall be no daydreaming, Lucius Junius Brutus," said Glyph. "You have much work to do before day's end. And there is still some kind of snake about. Never forget about that."

"How did you know I was daydreaming?" Lucius said.

Glyph simply smiled, the first time he had done so all day.

Lucius took a piece of bark from the pile on the right, wondering what writing and reading had to do with battling a prodigy. After all, he had defeated it and survived. He rubbed his skinned knuckles.

All right, he thought, as if his genius reminded him: barely survived.

And he began to copy.

::X::

The next morning Glyph announced that the snake had been defeated.

"When?" asked Lucius.

"Last night," said Glyph, and said nothing more. His voice was hoarse, and there were dark circles under his eyes.

Logophilus shared a look with Lucius, but he did not speak either. *How easy it is for Glyph to say nothing*, thought Lucius. Would explaining a thing take too long? He didn't suppose so.

They all scooped porridge for a moment, and finally Lucius said, "Glyph, how long will it be before I am a priest? I mean, a priest like you, fighting prodigies on my own?"

Glyph scraped his bowl, then locked eyes with Lucius, until Lucius looked away. "That is hard to say," he said. "But in a few years, you will know quite a bit."

"A few years?" said Lucius. "But I was in the portal yesterday. I perfected grammar."

"You were lucky."

"But I must become a priest before a year is up. I must

show King Tarquin."

"What, a year?"

"King Tarquin said that he would recall me after a year, and if I didn't show my worth to the Roman state, he would make me into a warrior."

Glyph said hotly, "Worth? Worth? The king doesn't know what worth is. He doesn't know what keeps him alive." It was as angry as Lucius had ever seen him.

"He thinks that I am sitting alone guarding tree bark."

"I know full well what he must think," said Glyph. "We have led him to believe..." He paused, then started again. "We have led all Etruscan kings of Rome to believe this. It is better. They sleep better. We are unmolested here."

"Nevertheless," said Lucius. "I cannot stay here. I am the king's nephew."

"You are half-Etruscan, yes," said Glyph. "That may be why you are so good at such a young age."

"Why is that?"

"The Etruscans have their own power. It does not come from grammarstones; it does not come from human language at all. It comes from a gift of reading nature."

"The *haruspices*-- the Etruscan priests?"

"They look at the flights of birds, the organs of slaughtered animals. They look into the hearts of men. Often they know what you are going to do before you yourself know."

"They do not use grammarstones?"

"No, they use mirrors. Anything that attacks them, receives the attack back upon them."

"So why cannot they fight the prodigies?"

"The *haruspices* do not use their power to attack, but to

defend. They would not go into a portal to detect what a prodigy is doing and fight it. They sit back, read their signs, and go into action only when forced. Even then, they believe that since they already have knowledge of their opponent and of the future, the matter is not a fight, but a kind of observation of what they already know will occur."

Lucius said, "This makes no sense to me. I think it is much better to make the first move, as we did today. If there is an enemy, attack him and do away with him."

"A mirror is not the same thing as a sword-- or even a grammarstone. But your opinion shows you are a Roman above all. We are people of action."

Lucius shook his head. He was learning much, and it was starting to make his head swim. He put his hand on Kaneesh's head, felt her warm, soft ears. This was, at least, something that he did not have to learn about.

In the distance, thunder rumbled.

Lucius looked up. Previously, the day had unfolded as had the others-- blue sky, almost no clouds. But now an apron of greenish vapor was passing over them.

Another rumble of thunder, and a distant flash of lightning.

"What is it?" Lucius said. They all stood up and Lucius dropped his bowl.

"The snake is not quite defeated," said Glyph.

The entire clearing was covered in the pale green cloud. Lightning flashed again, and thunder bellowed, and it began to rain.

But the rain was no rain.

It was snakes.

They fell on the trees, on the ground, in the vegetable

71

patch, on the roof of the *casula*. They were fat, long, gray with black stripes, and each one had a wet, hissing mouth and fangs. Lucius only had enough time to get underneath the threshold of the hut before it seemed as if there were snakes everywhere.

"*O murus Romaneis... circumventus,*" *I summon a wall for Romans surrounding,* Glyph said, letting go a grammarstone, and out of nowhere appeared a wall twelve feet tall and made of close-knit brick. "*O tectum Romaneis... supernum.*" *I summon a roof for Romans, above.* And they were covered with a strong roof of planks and beams.

Snakes hit the roof with a thump. Inside, the snakes that had already fallen were making their way to Logo, Lucius and Glyph.

Lucius' mouth was clamped shut; he couldn't have spoken a word of fear, much less a grammar. He backed away along the wall of the hut, his eyes fixed on a snake that had seemed to pick him out. The snake hissed and reared. Just as it was about to strike, Lucius felt the smooth handle of the axe that Logo used to split firewood. Without thinking, he snatched it up and brought the blade down on the head of the snake, cutting it in two.

Kaneesh had one by the neck. Logo came from inside the hut with a hunting knife.

"*securs serpentiis laminad celerrima,*" said Glyph. *The axe against the serpent with a blade... as swift as possible.*

The axe flew out of Lucius' hands. It whirled about their walled-off area, slicing snakes by itself. In no time all the snakes-- there were a dozen or more of them-- were dead.

"Good thinking, Lucius," said Glyph, out of breath.

"I didn't think. I just did it."

"Exactly what I mean."

"What about the snakes outside? What about the goats?"

"That is what we must do next."

The rain of snakes had stopped-- that was clear because there was no more thumping on the roof Glyph had made. Glyph made a window in the wall: *O fenestra muri quadrata... I summon a window in the wall, square.* Then he sent the axe through the window, *ventod, by the wind,* and it began doing its work on the remaining snakes. But when the handle snapped and the blade stuck in the ground, there were still many snakes left, and they were slithering up toward the window.

Glyph had been leaning on the window, and now he stumbled back. Lucius caught sight of Glyph's eyes. They were wild, wide, blood-shot. Kaneesh jumped into the gap and got a snake in her jaws, worried it, and threw it back down. Glyph went down on one knee. He held out the cane.

"Take this," he said. "I cannot--" and he leaned over and threw up the porridge he had eaten.

"Take it," yelled Logo. "Lucius, you can do it. Take the cane."

Lucius rushed over to Glyph, and wiped the porridge from his mouth. He could feel Glyph's breathing coming ragged and shallow. "He's alive!" Lucius cried.

Kaneesh growled and snapped at another snake.

"Take the cane," Logo pleaded. "Leave the master. Go. You can do it."

Lucius picked up the cane by the skinny end. A grammarstone, thank the gods, was already chambered in the knob. At least he had one chance to perfect a grammar.

Kaneesh jumped down from the window. She was taking

73

the fight to the enemy. She wasn't an Etruscan, waiting for the enemy to come and bounce off a bronze mirror.

Lucius climbed onto the window sill. Outside, the land was alive with snakes. Kaneesh snapped and barked at the snakes round about them, holding their ground, hissing, looking for their moment to strike. He dropped down next to her and swiped at the snakes with the cane.

What grammar to try? Lucius' mind was a blank. It had been easy when there was one snake, inside a portal. But what could he do that would stop one hundred snakes, a thousand snakes?

He heard Glyph's voice then: *the grammar is only the tool for your imagination.*

So few words came to him. *Aqua... ventus... lapis.... manus...*

Ignis?

Fire. Fire would kill the snakes. And it would destroy everything else with it.

Aqua?

Summoning great water might drown you, Glyph had said. Hercules had done it-- to clean the Augean Stables with its herd of magical cattle, he dug a great trench and diverted a river.

But there was one thing Lucius would add: let the water hug the ground. There would be no drowning then.

"*O aqua magna serpentiis... terrai.*" *I summon great water against the snakes... on the ground.*

And he let fly the grammarstone in the direction of the curtain of water near Glyph's cave.

At first there was nothing, only more snakes round about them, and Kaneesh next to him, her jaws foaming and her teeth bared.

Then a snake struck, Kaneesh yelped, and shrunk back. Lucius brought down the cane on the snake's back, and it let go of Kaneesh.

Then, there was a rumble like thunder, and a spray of water flew up from a group of boulders set in the direction of the curtain of water. Then a sheet of water, about as deep as one's knee, broke over them and swept all the snakes in its wake.

Lucius lost his footing and fell in the water. The face of a snake passed close to him, its green eye shiny, unmoving. Water and mud surged into his mouth. He was about to be carried off with it when a hand caught him-- Logo's.

The water kept coming as Logo hauled Lucius up into the window. "Well done," said Logo into his ear. He had already lifted Kaneesh to safety.

"The cane!" screamed Lucius, realizing he had lost hold of it. It had been washed up against the stone wall of the vegetable patch, and was pinned against it in the flood, like a piece of driftwood.

"I'll get it," said Logo, but Lucius was away in a second and floundering in the swift current. Again he was upended with a splash, and rode on his bottom toward the stone wall. He managed to stop himself from going over the wall, but the current was so strong, he knew that unless the water eased, he would not be able to move.

Lucius held on, and still the water came. He remembered the River Tiber. He had experience with swift water. This gave him some courage. He tried to get a foothold, slipped in mud, but was able to transfer one hand over the other, to get closer to the cane.

He did this several times, until he was quite close. But he could not make the last transfer of hand, to grasp the cane.

Logo said, "You're near enough. Perfect the grammar!"

Lucius opened his hand. "*Baculum... mani iuvenis...*" he managed to say. *Cane, in the hand of the young man.*

The cane leapt into his hand.

He chambered a grammarstone, let it fly, and said, "*aqua terrai... nulla.*" *Water on the ground... none.*

The flood eased, then stopped. The water receded. In a few moments, Lucius was holding on to a stone wall, dripping, his feet plunged into mud.

The vegetable patch was a mess. Almost all the plants were either covered in mud or swept away. The goat pen was gone. So were the goats.

The sun came back strong, and steam began to rise from the ground, as after a sudden, brief summer storm.

"*Gratulationes!*" yelled Logo, applauding. "Congratulations!"

Glyph's head appeared just above the window sill. He called to Lucius, unsteadily, but clearly. Lucius came, one sandal off, lost in the flood. Logo hauled Lucius up through the window. Kaneesh lay inside the conjured shelter, unmoving.

"The cane," said Glyph. He took it, touched Kaneesh with it. *Venenom cani... solutom*, he whispered. *May the poison in the dog be weakened.*

The dog was able to stand up. Glyph leaned over her. She licked his face.

"We need to get him in bed," said Logo. "He is older than you think."

They carried him through the window, and put him in Logo's bed.

"He is exhausted," said Logo. "Nothing else. His heart is very old."

"What shall we do with this new house?" Lucius asked, motioning to the wall and roof that Glyph had made.

"You will need to knock it down with grammar," said Logo. "Unless you have another axe."

"Can we keep it up for now?" said Lucius. "In case of more snakes?"

"For now," said Logo. "Yes, that it is a good idea."

::XI::

The next weeks passed quietly. No one saw a prodigy, not in the village, nor in the quarry portal.

"The *magus magister* has spent his strength," Glyph said one night soon after. "He was hoping to destroy you, Lucius. Because he knows you are strong."

Glyph had recovered, but had lost some of his strength. He leaned on his cane more when he walked, and he spent more time sitting next to the fire in the morning, collecting his thoughts.

At night, Lucius had dreams of snakes. But these made him less afraid than those about Glyph: Glyph falling from a great height, Glyph being swept away in a wind, Glyph being bitten by many snakes.

Once he said to Logophilus, "Can you teach me how to perfect grammar?"

Logo said, "I know a little. But I am like a tuft of grass, and my master is like a mighty oak tree."

Logophilus spent his time restoring the garden, the stone

wall, and welcoming a new herd of goats, supplied by the villagers. Glyph brought down the conjured wall and the roof by grammar, and Logo used the bricks to make a pavement outside the *casula*. The wood was cut into firewood, once a new axe was obtained, also from town.

"That old axe needed replacing anyway," Logo said.

Lucius studied diligently. Every time he became bored with the copying, or his hand cramped from writing, he remembered the panicked moment when he had had to think of a grammar by himself, using his imagination, and no words came to him. The thought of the Augean Stables had come to him only because the legends of Hercules were his favorites, and he had learned them all by heart from Demetria, whose aunt had told them at the loom day after day, in time with the winding and unwinding of the distaff.

Hercules had saved him that day. Now it was up to him to learn, as Glyph said, and never to be afraid again in battle, never to doubt that he was going to win.

And he studied ever more eagerly because of what Logo had said about Glyph: "He is older than you think."

One day after Lucius had learned all his letters, Glyph found him trying to spell words that Lucius thought would help him in battles with prodigies.

"*Hasta*, spear. *Gladius*, sword. *Clipeus*, shield," Glyph read. "These may help when you summon them. But summoning takes grammarstones, and it taxes the heart. What can you do with things that are already there? Look at your companions. If you want to bind an opponent, can you think of what you could do with a tree root?"

They discussed, and Lucius came up with *radics arboris*

serpentem religans, Root of a tree binding a serpent tight. Glyph made him copy that twenty times.

Lucius also learned how to make grammarstones, something Logo was charged to do when not keeping the *casula* and the cooking fire and the garden, along with the goats fed and milked and cheese made. They took chunks of rock from the quarry-- Glyph showed Lucius what kinds were the best-- and used a knapper, a bladed tool, to chip them into rough cubes. Then they sat down at a moving wheel made of stone and powered by a foot treadle, and ground down the cube until it was spherical and the proper size to fit into the cane.

Logo was able to make a grammarstone in less time than it took for water to boil in his tripod cauldron, but when Lucius tried to do it, the cube took forever to be ground into a sphere.

"You will learn," said Logo. He would take the dust from the grammarstones, throw it up in the air, and say, *o ignis lapidi, I summon fire in the stone.* And the dust would pop and sparkle and flare.

But he was always sure to do this when Glyph was not present.

And so it went. Lucius spent his days studying and copying Latin grammar, grinding grammarstones, practicing with the cane, and now and then going into the portal to scout. The caverns were large and winding, and he had a good idea of his way through there even in the dark after a while.

Other days, Lucius would help Logo in the garden, or walk with him to the village to ask news and bring back necessary things such as salt, sausages, or pieces of cloth or leather for mending clothes or equipment. Lucius did his laundry in the curtain of water, washing out his clothes and the cloak he slept in. He gathered bark from trees on which to write, and from time to time went into the woods with Kaneesh to hunt birds, using a grammarstone as he would in a sling, to strike and bring down the bird. Doing this helped him with the cane, until letting a grammarstone fly was second nature.

The hottest part of the summer passed over them, and for nine weeks, there was not even the rumor of a prodigy.

Then one day, when Logo went in to the village on his own to ask of news, he came back with a different tale.

Lucius had made the meal for that day: roasted quail that he and Kaneesh had hunted, with flatbread and fresh yellow beets rolled in salt. Logo had come back with pears, for it was beginning to be the season, and sour wine for pickling vegetables.

Glyph was cutting slices of pears for the others as Logo spoke, but he stopped when Logo gave his news.

"We are to have a visit," he said. "The villagers told me there is a trio of *haruspices* in town this week, a woman and two men, asking after the shrine of Numa Pompilius. As the people have never been here, and the place is a secret, they could not give directions. The Etruscans are in a foul mood, and are minded to stay until they find the answer."

Glyph said, "And they will find it, for knowledge to them is like water to the sea. The question is, why would they want to find us? They have their own affairs, and they have not been disturbed by prodigies as far as I know."

"Knowledge. Hmmmpf," said Logo. "Cooking fires are not hard to spot if you are looking for them." And he looked up at the trail of fat-laden smoke coming up from their own fire.

"Are they looking for a fight?" asked Lucius.

"I would be very surprised if they were," said Glyph.

"I think rather than let them come to us, we should go to them," said Lucius. "If they are enemies, this is the best way of dealing with them."

"Lucius has a point," said Glyph, as he cut a slice of pear into Logo's hands. "I have not been to the village for some time now, and I could use a visit. If the people do not see me for enough time, they start to tell outlandish stories about me being a spirit rather than a human being. And that is not good for anyone."

So it was decided. The next day they put on their sandals and Logo and Glyph their wide-brimmed travelers' hats, left Kaneesh to guard the goats and the vegetables, and set out just after dawn.

It was another fine day, fair except for a few clouds, jumbles of white-blue sky wool away off toward Rome and the sea. Soon the weather would turn. There would be the grape harvest, and a great festival at Rome, and soon after that rain for the first time in many a month.

They walked up to the ridge with the lopped fig tree, and followed for some time the path that Lucius had taken from Rome. They descended from the dry scrublands into meadows, and took a right turn onto a path that was hidden between stands of tall grass.

The path led to fields: grapes, hay, and vegetable patches protected by stone walls. Farmhouses, not much bigger than their own huts, roofed with thick masses of grass, began to appear. Here and there a cow, and more goats and pigs.

At every farmhouse a dog and a little boy or girl sat in the dust in front of the porch. The child would point and the dog would prick up its ears at the sight of the three travelers, and both would fall in with them as they walked.

"Who are you?" said each one of the children to Lucius as they came near, for they already knew Logo and Glyph.

"I am Lucius," said Lucius.

Before long there were so many dogs and children following them that when the question was asked, the rest answered for Lucius.

Before long they were at a crossroads, with houses on all four sides, the biggest of which had a stone porch, and two pillars holding up a stone lintel.

"This is the home of Gaius Terentius Celer," said Glyph. "The man of greatest respect in the village of Portentia."

One of the children, a boy not older than six, ran up to the door and flung himself into banging on it.

"They're here, they're here!" he shouted.

Out came an old woman, as slow as could be, her hands sticky with bread dough. She came out into the sun, frowned at the children and dogs and told them to shoo, flinging her hands at them so that bits of dough went flying and the dogs snuffled on the ground for them.

They did not leave, but shied back and formed a semi-circle around the travelers at their back.

Glyph said, "*Salve, Terentia mater*," and took her hand.

She glared at the kids, but when she turned her face to Glyph it was kind. She smiled, showing she had a few teeth left.

"Come in," she said. "My man is waking from his morning nap."

Celer, which means "The Swift One," was not to be rushed.

Terentia took them through the house to a pleasant garden with trees shading, where they sat on wicker-seated wooden benches. A servant girl, who turned out to be their niece, brought them wine and pears, and Glyph rubbed his weary legs.

The servant girl was about Lucius' age. She stared at him, but said nothing. Lucius realized he hadn't seen anyone but Logo and Glyph in months, and stared back. She seemed to take this as interest, and gave him a grin. Lucius blushed and looked away.

Logo said, "Remember that a priest of Numa takes no wife."

Lucius gave Logo a rough look. "I do not trifle with girls," he said.

Glyph said, "Hush."

Celer appeared, shuffling on a bad leg. He was squat and bald, but his eyes were strong and searching. He stared at Lucius, looking him up and down.

"Is this the new priestling?" said Celer gruffly.

"*Salve* to you, old man," said Glyph. "Are you quite awake?"

Celer waved Glyph off. "Who are you calling old man, old man?"

And they embraced, slapping each other's backs.

"Suddenly it is a busy summer," said Celer, after introductions were made. "Visitors every day."

"We heard that Etruscans are in Portentia," said Glyph. "Can we meet them?"

"I know that you do not come to see me, old friend," said Celer. "Would you not rather speak of the weather and the coming grape harvest? We think it will be a good one, apart from the field that was ruined by the blood rain."

They sat and spoke about grapes, and in between the visitors heard that the *haruspices* were out inspecting the dead field.

"Why do the Etruscans come here? They have no business with prodigies," Logo asked.

"I rather think they do," said Celer. "They asked many questions. I had no reason to lie. It has taken some time for them to take notice of our Roman powers and strangeries. But now that they have done so, I think they mean to conquer Portentia and the shrine the way they did Rome."

"You have spoken a true word," said Glyph.

"But why now?" said Logo.

Celer and Glyph glanced at Lucius.

The *haruspices* returned in time for the noon meal, and Celer had a goat prepared for them and the Romans. The servant girl and others from Celer's family set out tables and wicker-seated benches in the garden, and they ate together, speaking nothing about any purpose of coming, for mealtime among all Italians is sacred.

The names of the *haruspices* were Turanquil, Repsuna, and Velthur. Turanquil was the woman. They were all about Logo's age, had seen many summers, but were still strong and vigorous, though their skin was pale. They were among the few in Rome who did not see to their own farms.

Lucius found himself dozing over the conversation, about lore and history and kinds of plants that made the best medicine. But he snapped awake when Turanquil asked the following question:

"Where do you train the boy to be a priest of Numa?"

Glyph said, "This is Roman business, I think, not Etruscan."

Repsuna spoke as if he knew what Glyph was going to say: "But Rome is of Etruria. We are one, man of letters."

"Not in all things."

"In this, we are," said Repsuna.

Velthur put up his hand. "If the priest does not want to reveal the secret, let him keep it."

"We will find the answer, nevertheless," said Turanquil. "As we read the signs."

"That is your right," said Glyph.

"But we would like to be invited there," said Turanquil. "We do not want to invade."

"There will be no invitation to the shrine of Numa Pompilius," said Glyph. "It is only for Romans, and besides, there is nothing of interest there for Etruscans."

"We think there is," said Repsuna. "This man, Celer, told us of a blood rain that ruined his grapevines. He said you were one to make sure the rain does not spread. We would like to know how you do this, and what danger there is to Rome of such things."

"There is no danger to Rome," said Glyph.

"Previously, we had heard rumors of these prodigies, and we used them to predict the future, but now we see that they are not just signs, but dangers, and there is a power here. A great power."

"A power to rival the power of Etruria," said Velthur.

"The power to rival is nowhere here," said Glyph. "There is no contention between Rome and Etruria here."

"But I do see it in this one's eyes," said Turanquil, and

pointed at Lucius. She brought a mirror from within the folds of her *palla*, a cloak over her long dress. It was bronze, highly polished, and so dark it was almost black.

"You have no need of that," said Glyph, sitting up and grasping the knob of the *baculum*.

"There is no harm in looking in the mirror, is there?" said Velthur. "It will show this one's true intent."

Glyph gave a quick shake of his head, but stared at Lucius for a moment, which made Logo stare as well.

Lucius had said almost nothing up to that point, having nothing to say, and in the habit of not speaking on his own in front of grown men. But now he said, "Do you mean to curse me with all your evil eyes?"

"Lucius!" said Logo.

"Calm," said Glyph.

"He is headstrong," said Turanquil. "You need no mirror to know that."

Glyph said, "Many of his age are headstrong. That is not unusual. What's more, he is under my care. You have nothing to fear from him."

"We do not fear," said Repsuna quickly. "But we see trouble in the future-- the power of this place combined with the spirit of this young one. He is a prince, the son of a princess, close in ancestry to the king himself."

Turanquil extended the mirror to Lucius by its handle. "Examine," she said. "The other side." And she turned it so the reflecting side faced the ground.

Lucius took the mirror. It was beautifully smooth, as if new, except for the grooves cut into the handle. The non-reflective side contained pictures, made by pouring hot metal into a mold that the artist had created.

"By Hercules!" Lucius said.

"Yes," said Turanquil. "It is he."

There was Hercules, locked in a battle with the Hydra, a many-headed snake that could not be killed by chopping its heads off-- new heads would grow out of the stump of the old.

"It is beautiful," said Lucius.

"Do you want it?" asked Turanquil.

Lucius looked up. Glyph seemed to be thinking very hard. His eyes were down and his chin rested on his fist. Logo was digging dirt out of a fingernail with his thumbnail.

"You know he is Etruscan?" Velthur said to Glyph. "His mother is of our blood."

Glyph's eyes flashed up for a moment, but he said nothing.

"If you want it, you only have to turn it on the other side, and give your image to it," she said. "We can teach you how. There your genius will be safe forever."

Finally Lucius said, "I cannot take it. It is yours, lady."

Turanquil tsked. "Of no matter, young man. It is yours." And she pushed her palm toward him, as if pushing the mirror.

Lucius put it back in her hands. It was as if someone else was doing it, for his heart was set on the mirror. "It is yours," he whispered.

Turanquil scowled, but took back the mirror and replaced it in the folds of her dress. "This is not ended, priest of Numa," she said. "We read the signs, and we know what is likely to happen, and what is unlikely to happen."

"It is well," said Glyph, and there was a tiredness and hoarseness in his voice.

Celer said, "Do you wish to stay tonight, guests?"

"We would be pleased to accept your hospitality," said Glyph. Walking home would have taken a great effort on his part.

"As would we," said Velthur.

Logo swallowed hard.

Celer said, "Well, then, I will prepare sleeping places for all of you. Would you be pleased, dear Logophilus, to play for us and sing a story tonight? The people of Portentia speak of nothing else."

Now it was Lucius' turn to stare at Logophilus. What else was he doing in the village when he came down here?

"I accept gladly," said Logo, though he did not seem as glad as his words.

Celer laughed and clapped twice. The family came to clear away dishes and cups, and the niece who had grinned at Lucius laughed with joy when Celer told them Logophilus would be performing that night.

Suddenly Lucius was jealous of this girl who spent her days serving in her uncle and aunt's house. He thought well that he must speak with her later on.

"You sing and play?" Lucius said to Logo when they had a quiet moment. "But you never do so at home."

Logo said, "Glyph told me not to. It is distracting."

Lucius shook his head. It was almost enough to make him forget that the Etruscans considered him a dangerous person.

If they only knew, he thought, that I am only dangerous to snakes. But then he remembered the words of his brother Marcus:

We will call upon you at the right time.

::XII::

The rest of the afternoon, in the heat of the day, was given over to quiet repose on the porch that surrounded the garden on three sides. The family brought bed frames that were laid with goatskins and coverlets, and Glyph had a long nap. Even Lucius lay down for a while and watched bees light on bright red poppies. The rest of the time he walked the village, and spent most of it with the children, who flocked and fawned about him, asking for stories and wanting to play games.

In the evening, a great bonfire was lit at the crossroads, and the whole village came out to listen to Logophilus.

Logo was transformed. He had put a fresh smear of scented oil on his face and hair, and he stood with a great instrument, a Corinthian four-stringed lyre, looking like pictures of Greek rhapsodes that were painted on the pottery of well-to-do Romans.

When Logophilus plucked the strings on the lyre, the crowd applauded and cried, "*Optime!*" *Excellent*, a frequent refrain as Logophilus sang for them.

Lucius knew some of the stories Logophilus told, and others not. But the best one was that of Hercules and Cacus, one that was told often in Rome, but not with such skill as Logophilus had:

Hercules was driving his cattle home
The cattle of Geryon, the prize steers
When he came upon a goodly meadow
At the foot of a hill, a hill that would be Roman

Some day, some day, chanted the people. *Some day it would be Roman.*

Pasturing his cattle, Hercules lay down for the night
In the fragrant grass and the wildflowers
And the stars sprang up to dance.

To dance in the night, chanted the people.

Then the son of Vulcan, the fire-breather
The belly-boiler, the spouter of smoke
Kakos by name, the Bad One, the roarer,

Cacus, Cacus, came the chant.

He came, a terrible monster,
Of great size and fearsome aspect
And stole the cattle of Hercules.
Stole them, stole them.

Logophilus went on to sing that Cacus concealed the tracks of the cattle by pulling them away by the tail so that their tracks were muddled. He put them in his cave, far above on the Aventine Hill of the place that someday would be Rome.

But Hercules found the cattle, for even though he was none too swift in the head, he saw the smoke of the fire-breathing monster coming from atop the hill, and climbed up to the cave, where he heard his cattle lowing in the darkness.

Cacus was afraid of the great hero Hercules. He stuffed a boulder in the entrance to the cave, huge and stuck so tightly that Hercules, try as he might, could not dislodge it.

So he climbed onto the top of the hill where there was a hole for the smoke from Cacus' mouth to come out.

"He's good, isn't he?" said someone in Lucius' ear.

Lucius turned, saw the servant-niece, and scowled. He'd been listening so intently to Logo that she had startled him-- but he didn't want to appear as if she'd done so.

"By Castor!" said the niece. "An evil eye as I have not seen! Do you mean to curse me?"

"Sorry," said Lucius. "He is still singing."

"Listen, then, if you wish."

"Do you not wish to listen yourself?"

"I have heard this more than once," she said. "He always chooses this when he performs." And she giggled to herself.

Lucius was annoyed with the girl, who may have been older than he, but not by much. She was dark, unlike her mother and sisters, who spent most of the time indoors, and her nostrils flared like a horse's, and she had a tooth missing that made her speech sibilant. Still, she had no trouble looking Lucius in the eye, and that reminded him of Demetria.

"What is your name?" he asked.

"They call me Callidia," she said. *Callida* meant "clever" in Latin.

"That's funny. They call me Brutus."

She laughed, and it was not a nice laugh. It was more of a horse snort.

"You are from Rome," she said. "I would like to go there someday. Will you take a wife in Rome when you are finished living with the Sage in the hills?"

Logo had said that the priest does not take a wife, but Lucius found himself wondering whether he would be an exception to the rule.

"Or..." she said, and turned half-profile to him, "Will you be living up there with your wife?"

"Do you think you can persuade me to ask for you from your father?" Lucius asked, for it seemed she was being very obvious and ridiculous.

"I have no father," she said. "And I would never try to persuade you. But if you wished. That's all."

Lucius said, "You are more annoying than a sister."

She laughed again. "I am not so clever! Of course you see that. And you are. But I know some things."

"Like what?"

"Like they want to kill you."

"They?"

"The seers of things to come. The ones you talked with this afternoon. I overheard them speaking in Etruscan. I understand because I was an orphan and served an Etruscan family in the city of Veii from very young. Only recently did my uncle fetch me back from the Etruscans."

"Is it so?"

"They gave no thought to me, stupid serving girl. But they were talking how best to make sure you never came back to Rome." And she grinned triumphantly.

"Thank you," Lucius managed to say. His lips had somehow become thick, and he swallowed.

She noticed his fear, and smiled the more. "Of course, I would not want to be married to a dead man. But maybe they want to kill you because you are powerful. And I would like to be married to a powerful man. Is it true that you are powerful? I hear you are going to be the next Sage who protects our village from prodigies. Is that true? My cousin, Matutina, says that a Sage does not marry. She says..."

Callidia's words blended into Logo's music and singing, and Lucius nodded at her, said thank you again, and began to walk around the semi-circle of people listening to Logo with his back to the fire. Where were the Etruscans now? What were they planning? Was Callidia right about their intentions? There was no reason to doubt her; why would she lie about such a thing-- to impress him? To make him afraid? She was too simple-- not clever enough-- to do such a thing.

The Etruscans were seated on low wicker chairs to the right of Logo. Lucius stopped behind a number of villagers standing opposite the Etruscans. The fire flickered on their faces. The woman, the *haruspica*, stared intently at Logo. Lucius had heard Etruscans were keen on Greek stories. The mirror she had offered him had had a story of Hercules on the back of it.

Lucius thought that he must act first. He must stop them before they got him. But how? He would not tell Glyph or Logo. Glyph was old and weak now; he might not be able to take on the *haruspices*. On the other hand, Lucius had been practicing and working. He understood Latin grammar better and better every day. He could put a grammarstone wherever he wanted it. At fifty paces he could throw it through a hole the girth of a flatbread disc.

The question was, which grammar to perfect? He had never tried one against a real person. Glyph had said the grammar could kill, it could do anything, he could be like a god. But could he do something to scare them away, perhaps? Lucius' blood raced in his temples. Possibilities and kinds flew into and out of his mind, as if their letters had wings.

Ignis... sanguinem... Fire... blood...

The first thing was to get the *baculum*. Glyph, sitting next to the *haruspex* named Repsuna, held it at his knee, his hand resting on the knob. The light of the fire shined on the bone, making it look like a gem, like yellow jasper. Lucius knew it had two dozen grammarstones in it, neatly stacked in the hollowed-out shaft.

When Logo finished, there was a huge roar of approval, and applause. Young men then came forward to dance, wearing Cacus masks, and Logo joined with others who played pipe.

Lucius knew the only way to get the cane without asking would be to take it from Glyph as he slept. After that, it would be up to him to devise the grammar that would defeat his opponents before they attacked him.

The night was a cool one; the heat of summer was giving way, slowly, to fall, and the evenings were the first to herald this change. Lucius pretended to be tired much before he was, and lay down to get some rest before he had to wake deep in the night. Two *haruspices* slept in the room near the front porch, with the *haruspica* in a separate bedroom. Lucius, Logo, and Glyph slept under the roof of the garden portico, wrapped in fleeces to ward off the little breath of chill that fall was bringing.

Glyph returned to the house soon after Lucius retired, and soon was snoring loudly. Music continued on in front of the house for some time, and Logo did not return until after it had stopped. Nevertheless, almost as soon as he had lain down, he too was snoring. In response, Lucius heard the *tu*, *tu*, of an owl, calling him, *tu*, *tu*, *you you*.

Lucius managed to sleep for a time, long enough that when he woke to the mournful song of a nightingale, he jerked up on his pallet, thinking that he had slept too late and lost his chance.

But the night was still deep; the nightingale's call told him that, and the deep, sweet breath of the garden flowers exhaled on him, their stems and roots rejoicing in their respite from the late summer heat.

Lucius lay back, let his heart rest for a moment after the moment of panic, and collected his thoughts. He still had no idea what he was going to do, but he knew he must do it.

Slowly he sat up again, listening for the breathing of his companions. Logo's snoring was loud. He had drunk much wine that night, and would be senseless yet for many hours. Glyph, too, seemed to be breathing evenly, with little crooning wisps of snores. Lucius stood up, leaving his cloak on the bed along with the coverlet. He shivered a little; it was that cool tonight, and his toes gripped the hard, beaten dirt of the portico. He dared not lean down to put on his sandals. The snap-snap of them as he walked would be too loud.

He crept forward, his eyes accustoming themselves to the near-blackness. The only light came from the stars and a crescent moon dipping now below the rooftree of the main house. This was good, Lucius thought. Darkness meant he would have the advantage; his eyes would be night-big, while anyone just waking up would see nothing.

Glyph lay on his side, the cane next to him, propped on the edge of the bed-frame. Lucius silently cursed his luck that it wasn't on the ground next to him. There would be a change when he took it. Even though Glyph was not holding it, it was near him, and the feeling of the cane was like a living thing. It was not warm so much as always moving back and forth, like a string on Logo's cithara, just plucked.

Lucius knelt, conscious that even his breath on Glyph's face could wake the old man. He reached out with both hands, and both hands touched the cane at the same time. That vibration in the cane reverberated throughout Lucius' arms, and he struggled to keep his breathing even and silent. He pulled the cane back toward him, slowly, slowly, and was pleased as he did that Glyph continued to give a whistle-snore at the same pace as when the cane was still there.

Lucius let the cane down on its tip end, and pushed himself on it to a standing position. It was good; he had the cane and Glyph was still asleep. He drew the cane up to his chest, and grasped it in ready position. Almost without thinking, he flicked the cane quickly, and a grammarstone clicked into position in the knob chamber.

Glyph snorted. He had heard the click in his sleep-- or had he? Lucius bit his knuckle and blamed himself for chambering a grammarstone too soon. But it was like second nature now. He could hardly stop himself.

Glyph snorted once again, then sighed and turned over, pulling the coverlet with its soft goat-fur closer to his neck. He grumbled something in his sleep that sounded to Lucius first like a groan, but then like *bona fortuna, good luck*.

Lucius moved away toward the threshold of the house. Now that he had a grammarstone loaded, he felt ready to devise a grammar. He first thought of summoning light, but discarded the idea. Then he thought of summoning silence, and spoke it in a whisper, kneeling, with his head close to the cane as he threw the grammarstone to the floor:

O silentiom pedebos et voci iuvenis

...I summon silence on the feet and the voice of the young man.

He had chosen "voice" at the last second, thinking it a good thing just in case he were to cry out or make some other inopportune sound.

The grammarstone hit the ground and split in two, then vanished. Lucius tried to scrape his feet, to see if the grammar was perfected. It was. His feet did not give a sound.

Then he tried to yell, and he felt the sound come up from his throat, but nothing went out into the air.

Perfect.

Confident, he walked into the deep darkness of the house, and even with his owl eyes, he could see almost nothing. He grasped for a wall as he came through the threshold, and kept to it, walking along it until he came to the right angle of another wall. Halfway down that wall, the sounds of the sleeping seers came to him.

They did not snore, but it was clear they were fast asleep.

Their breathing was shallow, coming in infrequent sighs.

"I will deal with them first," Lucius said to himself, pleased that when he whispered, there was no sound at all.

He chambered another grammarstone with the tiniest of clicks-- maybe he should've made some kind of silence around the cane as well, he thought too late-- and raised it, thinking on what would be the best kind of fate for men who were plotting to kill him.

With the cane raised for what seemed like a long time, it came to Lucius finally that there was no reason to kill them. Blinding seemed best-- what could a blind man do to one who could see?

Slowly the grammar formed in his throat: *nocs oculeeis haruspicis sempiterna... May eternal night lie on the eyes of the seer.*

He let the grammarstone go, but there was a problem.

No sound came from his throat.

And then the next problem: the grammarstone never hit his intended target, the second *haruspex*. Instead, it hit the mirror of the *haruspica*.

He knew it hit the mirror, because when it hit, the mirror lit up, and the whole room lit up in its glow, and he saw the *haruspica* holding the mirror, her graying hair unpinned and flowing down onto her shoulders and framing her face, wrapped in a cloak for sleeping that went down to her ankles. She looked a statue, with a little smile like that on a marble Greek goddess. It was as if she had known exactly where Lucius was going to throw the stone, and blocked it with the mirror, with no effort at all.

Now the grammarstone came flying back at him, faster than he'd sent it, and he ducked just in time. It cracked against the plastered wall and embedded itself in it.

Lucius gasped, but made no sound. He looked around. There was Glyph in the threshold.

"*Baculum mani litterarii ventod*," he said. *The cane in the hand of the priest by the wind.*

The cane flew out of Lucius' hands, and stuck in Glyph's. He chambered a stone and raised it, and for a moment Lucius thought he must have been readying another grammar, this one against the *haruspica*.

But Glyph said nothing, and the *haruspica* said nothing, and slowly the glow began to fade from the mirror, like a fire losing its life.

The *haruspica* held her mirror out to Glyph, reflective side out, just in case Glyph decided to attack her, but he didn't. He motioned to Lucius, cane still up, then told him to get behind him.

"We have no quarrel with you, lady," said Glyph finally.

"But he must," she said, pointing the mirror at Lucius.

"He is a fool. We call him Brutus."

She laughed, and kept the mirror up. "Let him look in the mirror and we will see if you speak truly."

"Let him try to speak. He cannot."

She straightened a little, and a frown came up on her face, but she stayed on guard.

Lucius put his hand to his throat. He tried to speak, felt the vibrations on his fingers. Nothing audible came.

"Lower your weapon, and I will lower mine," she said. "You have nothing to fear from me, if indeed you have no evil intent yourself."

Glyph put down the cane. She lowered the mirror.

"I wish you good sleep," she said. She looked down at the other two seers, still asleep, and laughed again. "These two. Worthless."

Glyph turned to Lucius, and said, "Out. I will speak to you when--"

But he didn't finish the sentence. There was a hissing sound, a thump, and he fell forward, collapsing into Lucius' arms. In the last glow of the mirror, Lucius saw, in Glyph's back, the hilt of a dagger.

::XIII::

Glyph let go of the cane, and Lucius caught it before it hit the ground. He whirled it around and chambered a grammarstone, but it was like a gash had been cut in his stomach and his insides were falling out.

The *haruspica* was rousing the other two Etruscans. She had one dagger and only one, or she would've thrown it at Lucius. Lucius took Glyph's head in his hands. A trickle of blood came from his lips, and his eyes were thrown up to the tops of their sockets.

Lucius tried to cry out again, but again, nothing came, and he realized that without his voice the grammarstones were useless, and even the grammarstones themselves couldn't hurt the *haruspica* if she could deflect them as easily as she had the first one.

So Lucius ran. He left Glyph and ran to Logophilus.

He tried to yell, "Logo, Logo, wake up!" But nothing came out, so he could only shake him.

102

Logo turned over and said something, maybe in Greek, Lucius couldn't quite tell, but did not rise. For a moment Lucius thought he might have to leave him as well, but with a last burst of inspiration he pulled on Logo's ear, and Logo screamed in pain, but woke.

"What?" he cried.

"Get up, get up, they're after us. We have to run," Lucius said silently.

"What? Who is it? Get your hands off me." Logo could not see Lucius in the black night. Without the ability to say anything, Lucius might as well have been a stranger.

Lucius said, "Please. We must, we must. Oh, by my genius."

But he heard nothing.

From across the garden the three Etruscans appeared in the light of oil lamps, making their way over the prone body of Glyph and into the portico.

"They killed Glyph! We must flee."

"What is going on? Who are they? Where is Glyph?" Logo sputtered, still heavy with sleep.

Lucius pulled Logo by the arm out of his bed and put the cane next to his hip. In the next instant there was the same hiss of the throwing dagger. It flew somehow between or around them and thudded into a wall, making a hollow "ting" sound as it did.

Lucius felt the cane being taken from him.

"*O fusca aeri Graeco et iuvenei*," said Logo, *I summon smoke in the air for the Greek and the young man*, and a cloud of thick white smoke immediately appeared in front of them, and all about them.

"Run," Logo urged, and they were off into the field behind

the house, skirting a heavy thicket of blackberry canes.

They ran for a long time without speaking, looking at each other, or looking behind them, until Lucius began to have a stitch in his side and to marvel at Logo's stamina. Then he realized Logo still had the cane, and that may have had something to do with it. They only stopped when they began to be in wild hill lands again, and there was no clear path to run along. Large stones, thorn-bushes, tall grass, and overhanging trees stood in their way.

The sun was beginning to gray the eastern sky. The moon was still above the hilltops over to the west. A breeze came up and bent the grass, and again, Lucius shivered.

"You can't speak, can you?" Logo finally said, after he had caught his breath.

Lucius tried again. No, he couldn't.

"What is it? What happened?"

Lucius pointed to the cane, then to himself, then put his hands in front of his face.

"You perfected a grammar... but you made a mistake?"

Lucius nodded his head vigorously, and tears flew from his eyes. He knelt down in the dust and pounded his fist on his chest. He couldn't sob or moan or groan. Tears simply streamed down, and he kept pounding his chest.

"And Glyph?"

Lucius screamed noiselessly, dug his fingernails into the ground, picked up handfuls of dust, and threw them in his face. He sat down and poured dust over his head, hitting himself now on the chest, now on the head.

Finally, Logo knelt next to him and took hold of his arm. His hand was strong and firm. He said nothing, but opened

Lucius' palm so that the dust fell out of it, and replaced the dust with his own palm. He held Lucius' hand, and put his arm around Lucius' shoulder. Lucius put his head next to Logo's, and they sat there for a long time, until the sun was teasing out long shadows from the trees and stones.

Presently there came a sound of something walking through underbrush. Then a bark, a yip, and a yowl.

"Kaneesh!" Lucius said, and this time he heard himself. His voice was hoarse and weak, but he rejoiced the grammar on it had worn off.

There was the dog, wagging her tail, tongue out and panting. She had come from some unseen path, and now brushed up against Lucius, and licked his face.

Immediately Lucius felt something like courage wash back into him. At least it was a feeling that he might go on, that he might get up from the dust.

"Let's go," Logo said. "Kaneesh will lead the way. We are safe for now. When we get back home we will see what we need to do."

When they arrived, after making their way through thickets and over hills, Logo made barley porridge, Lucius ate a little, and then lay down on his bed and slept, no dreams. At noon he woke, and it was silent, and he remembered Glyph again, and tears flowed.

Logo came into the hut and gave Lucius a scroll.

"Glyph wrote this after the snake attack," he said. "He told me to give it to you if he died before you went back to King Tarquin."

Lucius beheld the signs, so beautifully put down on the skin as to bring to mind immediately the kind, intent face of Glyph bending over it in lamplight, scratching with the stylus and leaving ink behind, then dipping more ink, and scratching again.

Lucius read what he could, and when he faltered over a word, Logo put it in for him.

To Lucius Junius Brutus, I, Publius Litterarius, give greeting.

If you are reading this, my dear child, it means that my spirit has gone to our ancestors.

Do not be sad, Lucius. This is the path we must all tread someday. I have lived longer than I deserved.

"No," Lucius said to himself. "You deserved to live, but my own foolishness brought your end."

Suppose for a moment, the letter went on, *that you feel my death somehow came because of you-- that you caused it, either because we worked too hard, or you brought me into undue danger.*

Do not think this. If death comes, it is because it is time.

And it cannot be undone.

Suppose for a moment that you feel you will not be able to become a priest without my help.

Do not think this either. You are already a priest. You have defeated a great prodigy.

When I said that it would take years before you would become a priest, I simply wanted you to be patient and learn. But sometimes we do not have the time we would like to have.

I have deliberately let your spirit rule the pace of your learning. I have let you go, I have let you take the bit in your mouth. But I have reined you in at the proper moment.

Now it is time for you to take the baculum *and the* lapides *and make of them what you will. No one is going to stop you but yourself. Logo will help as he can to see you on the right path. He can do a few things, and can teach you a few things, for it is difficult not to learn when you spend time with the grammarstones.*

But do not look to Logo as a teacher. Instead, ask him for what you need, and take it if he has it.

I think that by the manner of my death, you will know what it is you need to do in order to protect Latium.

The last thing I will advise you, however, is that you hide your power. Do not let the Etruscans know about it. Do not attack them and they will not attack you. Rise up in power and they will rise to bring you down. Wait; gain strength from battling the prodigies. There is no fruit in rashness.

I bid you farewell, dear child. You will always be in my heart. You will have the strength of the ancestors and your genius beneath you, above you, and at your back.

Vale. Farewell.

::Glyph::

It was some time before Lucius could bring himself to tell Logophilus the whole story, but as the afternoon sun lengthened the shadows again, and as Lucius sat with Kaneesh at his feet, and Kaneesh's soft ears at his hand, he spoke.

"A serving girl told you she had overheard the Etruscans plotting your death?" Logo said. "How did you know she was telling the truth?"

"I didn't," Lucius whispered, and bitterness soured his voice.

"You were frightened, but you thought it best not to speak with us."

"I thought I could defeat them myself." Lucius picked up a

rock and cast it into the woods. "It didn't seem as if it would be difficult. Not then."

"You took the cane?"

"Glyph was asleep."

"He would not have let you take the cane unless he wanted you to," said Logo. "Glyph sleeps very lightly."

"It seemed as if he said something," Lucius said. "He turned over and said something like *bona fortuna, good luck.*"

"He let you go," said Logo. "He must have decided to let you make your own decision."

Lucius thought of what Glyph had written: *I have let you go, I have let you take the bit.* And then, when he came in behind Lucius, that must have been what he considered the proper moment.

"I designed a grammar that would blind the two men. I thought that was clever, to make blind the ones who see the future.

"But first I thought it even cleverer to put a grammar on myself for silence."

"And you shut your own mouth."

"I never thought--"

"Which is why it were better that you come to us first," said Logo.

Lucius only shook his head, his stomach expanding up to his heart and lungs, making it difficult to breathe. His head swam with images, memories, what Glyph had said, and with the sight of the *haruspica*, her mirror glowing from contact with the grammarstone.

Kaneesh barked.

"What?" Lucius said. They both got up, as Kaneesh leapt

away along the path to the cut fig tree.

Logo said, "We have visitors."

"If it is the Etruscans--"

"Ready the *baculum*," said Logo. "But do not attack them directly. They will use the mirrors against us if so. Think about how we can defeat them without fighting them."

"How is that possible?"

"Design your grammar," Logo said, and followed Kaneesh into the woods.

Lucius came behind, cane in hand, a grammarstone chambered, wondering what he could design that would defeat the Etruscans, but not affect him.

Ventus... wind... manus... hand...

Kaneesh had waited for them by the stream from the spring. Now she sprinted ahead. Logo stepped quickly, bent over, up the grade to the ridge. Lucius followed, the cane poised above his head.

Kaneesh stopped and pricked up her ears just before the crest of the ridge, near the tree that Logo had climbed on the day Lucius arrived. Logo came up to the trunk and flattened himself against it. He motioned to Lucius to kneel.

Spes... hope... sanguis... blood...

Kaneesh gave a yip, and flashed forward.

No, thought Lucius. *They'll kill you. They have daggers, and they throw them end over end-- into your back.*

Then he heard a voice he thought he recognized. Against his will he stood up, and saw the crown of someone's head, with black curls cascading down from it.

"Dog," said the voice. "You are back! Did I follow you wrongly? Where are we going, you little rascal?"

Lucius raced up the ridge. There, in the fading sunlight, was someone he had not expected to see.

"Lucius!" cried Demetria.

::XIV::

She looked much older. It had only been a few months, but she seemed much taller, her neck longer, her cheeks thinner. She had always been round in the face, because her mother fed her well and used to give her flatbread soaked in honey and olive oil. Her father always had much oil because he traded wool for it overseas, and Romans brought them honey to pay for the beautiful fabrics her mother made.

As they had gotten older, Demetria began helping herself to the treat. Many had been the day that Demetria would meet him behind her house, running with a big, wet flatbread that she would tear in half and give to him from her sticky hand.

Now here she was, slender and boyish, with a *petasus*, a traveling hat, on a strap around her neck. She was wearing a long traveler's robe, leggings, and sandals, looking for all the world like a merchant's assistant, a Greek who helps his master bring out the choicest of the wools for his customers.

But even in disguise, there was no mistaking that troublemaker's grin.

"How?" Lucius began, but Logo stepped forward and put his hand up to silence him.

"*Chre ou einai tode se*," he said. It was Greek, which Lucius understood a little. But the tone of the voice was unmistakable. He knew her, and was annoyed to see her.

"Uncle," she said, and motioned to Lucius, as if apologizing for using Latin, "I need to talk to him."

"Uncle?" Lucius said, and stared at Logophilus.

Logo went on in Greek. He clearly wanted her to leave. He kept pointing back to Rome. She answered in Greek, flushed, shook her head, pointed at Lucius.

"You cannot be here," Logo finally said in Latin.

"Can I at least give him my message?"

"We may not have time," said Logo. "I told you, it's dangerous."

Lucius thought it was a good sign that they had switched to Latin. Maybe it meant that he could say something now.

"Logo, if she has a message for me..." Lucius said.

Logo stood between them and twined his arms over his shoulders. "Then she needs to speak it and be off."

"But it is getting late. I won't make it back to Rome before nightfall," said Demetria. "I will have to sleep out, or walk in the dark. And my legs are tired. It was a very long way, uncle."

"There is a moon tonight."

"Logo, what harm is there in letting her stay a night?" Lucius said. "The Etruscans--"

"Don't speak of the Etruscans."

"But that is part of my message," Demetria insisted. "It is a matter of life and death, Lucius."

"We know that," said Logo. "We have just been down in

the village and made enemies and we know they want us dead."

"No. I have other news. Please. It's important."

"Logo," said Lucius. He put his hands out, palms up. "By my genius."

Kaneesh barked and wagged her tail furiously, and took a few steps down toward the spring and the house.

"So you think she should come as well, do you, dear girl?" Logo said. "This is a terrible business. If only Glyph were here."

And so Logophilus was convinced. They went down, Logo muttering all the way in Greek, Kaneesh running ahead, then circling back with an impatient bark.

"How we've missed you!" Demetria said as they walked. "The boys' council is in chaos without you to calm them all down. "

"How do you know what the boys' council does?" Lucius said.

She grinned. "Do you think there are no ways to get close to the council without being seen?"

Demetria went to wash her face, hands and feet in the curtain of water, and Logo and Lucius set about making a meal for her. When they had eaten, and the sun was setting and a good fire going, she spoke her news.

"Lucius, I'm sorry to have to tell you this," Demetria said. "Tarquin has sent your brother to war. He's an officer in a corps of cavalry to fight against the Volscians."

"The season of war will soon be over," said Logo. "A few more weeks of good, calm weather. Winter will be here sooner than we think."

Demetria said, "I heard from some of the soldiers they are

going to Suessa Pometia."

"It is a great city, richer than Rome," said Logo. "It used to be a colony of Alba Longa, an ancient city that had its hey day before Rome was born. But it fell into the Volscians' hands."

"If it is richer than Rome, then they must have an army to defend it," said Lucius.

"The soldiers seemed to think that victory would be easy," said Demetria.

"They always do-- before," said Logo.

"Well, may it be easy," said Lucius. "For my brother's sake."

"But you said before that Lucius' life was in danger," Logo said.

"Yes, ah, well," Demetria said, and her eyes fluttered for a second. "It is in danger... I mean... in the sense that Lucius' brother is a part of Lucius himself."

Logo snorted. "This is how you convinced me to bring you here?"

"I had to say something. You were going to send me away to walk all night back home. And mother and father will be furious with me, even so."

"But, you stupid girl, don't you understand that you are in danger here? We are being hunted."

Demetria said, "I think you are well hidden. I don't even know how I was able to come as far as I did. The dog--"

"Kaneesh," Lucius put in.

"Yes, Kaneesh. She saved me. I was lost. I don't think I could've made it back to Rome."

"You foolish, foolish girl."

"We cannot quarrel over this anymore," Lucius said. "She is here, and that's that." He tried to make it sound like something

Glyph would say-- something wise and fair-- but secretly he was pleased. He had wanted for so long to tell Demetria about the signs, the kinds, the possibilities, the companions. He said, "Maybe this is an opportunity for her to learn grammar, to help us. We will need help, I think."

"There is only one *baculum*," Logo pointed out.

"True enough," said Lucius. He stole a look at Demetria, who was staring at him. "But she might use it, if I..."

"She is Greek, as well," said Logo. "To use the full power of the grammar, you must be Roman."

Lucius said, "At least she might..."

Logo waved his hand in front of him. "If only Glyph were here!"

Lucius and Demetria took this as approval, and Lucius invited Demetria down to the cave, telling Logo they'd be back soon. He used a grammar to separate the curtain of water, and went into the scroll room where Lucius lit several oil lamps.

Demetria's eyes shined in the flickering light, beholding the stacks of skins, the table with stylus and ink, and the stack of bark on which Lucius had written.

"It is the place of Numa, truly," she whispered.

Wordlessly, he took her hand and gave her a scroll to open, the first scroll of kinds and possibilities from which he had learned to read. They opened it together, each with a hand on either side, and she smiled widely and said, "*Nuna demuna*," which in their private language had meant, "Secret writings."

She ran her fingers over the smooth surface of the skin. "It looks like Greek. Look, here is alpha, and here is an epsilon, and an iota. But here is one I have not seen," and pointed at a Q.

"We can read this, just like Greek," said Lucius. "But it is Latin."

Demetria opened the scroll further, and pointed to a word, as if about to ask what it was, but a spot of wet appeared next to her finger. She looked up. Lucius' eyes were bright with tears.

"What is it?" she asked.

"My teacher," he said.

They embraced. They had never done so before. There was no reason to, as far as Lucius was concerned. But now they were both older; he was a man, and she, well, she seemed to have grown up, too.

They held each other a long time before she whispered, "I missed you."

Lucius nodded. "And I you," he said. He drew himself away, wiped his face, and thought for a moment. "I wish you could have come with me."

"Your teacher?" she said, taking his hand.

He rested it in hers, and said, "Gone. I knew him for so little time. And learned so much. But now I must be the teacher."

"I will learn from you. Whatever it is."

"It is important."

"I know."

Then Lucius almost said something he hadn't ever thought about saying to a girl-- or a woman-- ever before. *Te amo*. I love you. But he didn't. Too much to think about. Too much after Glyph, after that night, the mirror, the *haruspica*, the dagger, the grammarstones, the silence on his voice. He would never make a mistake like that again. Glyph had told him he now had the power of the *baculum*. He must use it wisely.

The *baculum*. He had set it down on a chair, and now he felt a buzzing, and a whirring. The cane was rolling, tumbling off the chair. Would it shatter if it fell?

"*Baculum mani iuvenis ventod*," *The cane in the hand of the youth by the wind*, he said. It leapt to him.

Immediately he knew something was wrong. The *baculum* vibrated in his hands.

"What is it?" Demetria said.

"Something... an enemy..." Lucius said, not knowing exactly what it was. But Kaneesh appeared from a hidden passageway and barked, and he heard Logo calling from outside.

"Lucius! A prodigy! Come quickly!"

They ran, passed through the curtain-- *aquam ventod*-- and Logophilus pointed up the stone stairs.

"One of the goats," he said, panting. "Had the face of a cow."

Lucius scrambled up the steps. He heard Logo say, "You stay here" to Demetria.

"No," said Lucius. "She is with me."

"She is not your wife," said Logo, balling his fist. But then he opened it, pleading. "It is dangerous. You know it is."

"But she must learn," Lucius said.

Demetria sidestepped Logo and joined Lucius, and together they ran up the steps hand in hand. Logo came behind, calling for them to watch their step.

It was nearly sunset, and the light had turned the quarry an eerie purplish-pink color.

"What is this place?" Demetria said, out of breath from the run.

"Prodigies," Lucius said. He looked up at the cliff face for the now-familiar opening to the prodigy cave. "Threat from another world."

"The Underworld? The land of death?"

"Similar to it," said Lucius, and perfected a grammar. *Iuvens et Graeca ventod volantees. The youth and the Greek girl flying by the wind.* He threw down a grammarstone, put his arm behind Demetria's back and clutched her hip. They rose up, the built wind raising a cloud of dust under them. Then he told the wind to place them on the ledge, and in a moment both were standing near the entrance to the cave.

"I can't believe it!" she cried, and whooped so that the echo ran through the quarry.

"Shhhh!" said Logo, beneath them.

"You don't have to go in," said Lucius. "If you don't want to."

"Do you not have a cane like that for me?"

"No, indeed," said Lucius. "But even if you do nothing, you will learn."

"And if I die, then I am not far from the Underworld!" Demetria said with a laugh.

"You won't die," Lucius said, remembering how Glyph had let him explore on his own that first day. Somehow he had known Lucius could do it. "Come on," he said. "I've been here many times."

Lucius sent a grammarstone down to create light, and the first chamber where he had escaped the great snake glowed. They floated down on the wind, *ventod levissimod, very gently*, and found themselves on the gravelly floor.

"I hear something," said Demetria.

It was so. From other chambers came an echoing clash and scrape of metal on metal.

"Through here," said Lucius. "Stay behind me. If we separate, we meet back here. If you don't see me for a time, climb back up the wall. You can do it. Like the Tarpeian Rock."

"I never got to do that. You silly boys never let me."

Lucius stepped through an opening in the rock wall and threw another grammarstone for light. Then he saw it.

Demetria was just behind him, stepping over the low rocks that made a kind of doorsill into the next chamber. She put her hand on his shoulder and peered into the cave.

"No," she whispered. "Not that."

::XV::

Before them stood a warrior, perhaps twice as big as a tall man in Rome. But it wasn't human. It seemed to be made of shiny-black bronze, and had six arms, three on each side. It was holding two swords, and four mirrors. Its helmet was of bronze, and its armor as well. But its face looked like...

"Marcus?" Lucius said.

The demon swiped with both swords, as if cutting grain with a scythe. Instinctively, Lucius put up the cane to block the blows, as he had done many a time when practicing swordsmanship.

There was a flash, a scream from Demetria, and one of the swords exploded in shards of metal. The cane flew out of Lucius' hand and rattled against the cave wall.

Lucius had almost no time to dodge the next swipe of the remaining sword, and as he did so, he bumped Demetria so that she stumbled against the rock threshold and fell back out of the cave.

"*Baculum mani ventod!*" screamed Lucius, and the cane flew to him again. He ducked against the cave wall as another blow came toward him and cut the bottom off his tunic and sliced into his leggings. A double sting told Lucius the sword tip had raked both thighs.

Lucius threw a grammarstone and said, "*Militem aeratom ignid liquifactom*," *Bronze soldier melted by fire*. But three mirrors came up to block the stone, and it glanced away with a plink, then came straight for Lucius. He ducked, the stone exploded against a cave wall, and a spout of fire came up, ultra-hot.

The demon-warrior stepped back for a moment, still holding up the mirrors for defense, as Lucius scrambled away and held the cane up. Lucius stood right next to the opening, to retreat if need be, but he was ready now, and was thinking furiously of his next grammar.

But then the monster did something Lucius was not expecting.

"Brother," it said, in Marcus' voice.

"What?" Lucius cried.

"What?" Demetria cried, and linked an arm around Lucius' chest. She had gotten up again and come behind him.

"Help me, Lucius," said the demon warrior. "I am in danger. Go to Suessa. You can defeat the army there. You can save my life."

Lucius took a step back. The backs of his sandals were just at the rocks at the floor of the opening. It would have been simple to tell Demetria to retreat, and then fly up and out of the cave. It would have been easier than facing a giant bronze warrior with two swords and three mirrors.

Marcus, or the face of Marcus, looked as if he was in pain. He groaned, and repeated that he was in danger.

121

"How do I know it's you?" Lucius demanded, the cane still raised.

"It's not Marcus," Demetria whispered. "It's trying to trick you."

"Brother," said Marcus, and groaned.

"What if it is a message from the gods?" Lucius said. His mind was wild with the thought that he might lose Glyph and Marcus, and both deaths would be his fault.

"It is a monster," Demetria said. "It wants to kill you."

"I..." Lucius began, but couldn't finish. The demon had been slowly closing the distance between it and Lucius, and now with a long arm, it brought down the face of a mirror on Lucius' head. It would have crushed him, had not Lucius interposed the cane at the very last moment, so that instead of smashing Lucius' brains out, the mirror exploded with a screeching clash of metal on bone.

Lucius fell forward and Demetria, clutching at him to keep him upright, instead fell on top of him. He tasted dirt and stone. He spit out a shard of gravel and rolled. She rolled with him, and he blocked a sword thrust, then took the cane in both hands and whacked at the mirror that came right after.

Another explosion. Lucius couldn't hear anything anymore, and he could hardly see for the smoke. Lucius ordered the wind to blow the smoke out of the opening, and when it did, the warrior with the face of Marcus had retreated to the opposite wall of the cave with one sword and one mirror left.

"By Hercules," Lucius said, panting, his nose filled with the bitter smell of hot metal and powdered grammarstone. "I know how to defeat you."

Then he spoke:

Baculum speculei penetrans
The cane in the mirror penetrating

The cane flew like a missile, and pierced the face of the mirror as the monster brought it up to defend. There was another deafening boom, and smoke, and it was a moment before Lucius saw that the cane had continued on through the mirror and had embedded itself between the eyes of the Marcus face.

The demon-warrior fell with a clash of bronze, the cane still sticking out of its head.

"My brother," Lucius screamed.

"It wasn't!" Demetria cried. "See!"

The face of the demon-warrior had changed. It was now nothing but twisted metal, like a bronze statue that had once had a lifelike face, but now, with a great hole in its forehead, looked nothing human.

Lucius moved to the *baculum*, but saw that it glowed hotly, and would burn him if he tried to touch it. In fact, the whole room was intensely hot; sweat was flowing down Lucius' face and into his eyes.

He turned to Demetria and embraced her again, his heart leaping up and down. Her hair, smelling singed and powdery, brushed the side of his face and ear. He blew a strand of it from his mouth, then felt something wet on his neck.

He took her chin in his hands, lifting it. A shard of metal protruded from her neck. A ribbon of blood trailed from the wound.

"By my genius!" Lucius said. "You're hurt."

She touched the metal, winced, and let herself down into a sitting position. "It's not... so bad," she said.

Lucius went back for the *baculum*. It was still hot to the touch, but he pulled it out of the bronze warrior's head, let it fall on the ground, shook his hands out to ease the burn, and picked it up again.

Gently lifting Demetria's chin, he touched the *baculum* to the protruding metal, which shriveled like a leaf and fell from Demetria's neck. She put her hand over the wound.

"*sanguis Graecais... incolums*," he said. *May the blood of the Greek girl be unharmed.*

He leaned over her to look more closely at the wound, which he thought he saw closing up. He felt Demetria's hand on his ear, and he looked up at her.

She kissed him.

It was on the lips and over almost before it started, and it tasted as the whole room must have, as sour as a blacksmith's workshop. But to him, he had never known anything sweeter.

"You will be the greatest man who ever lived," she said.

As they waited for the cane to cool down, a shyness came to them. Lucius helped her up, and they dusted themselves off.

"I'm sorry," he said. "If you were scared."

She laughed, shakily, but even so, she laughed. "Nothing is more frightening than my father when he is angry," she said. "This..."

"I just wanted you with me."

"I didn't DO much," Demetria said. The glow of the grammarstone was now fading in both chambers.

"You told me about Marcus."

"I have had such dreams, of strange faces on strange bodies. The face of my mother on a cow. It was after my aunt told me the story of Io."

Lucius smacked his hands together in recognition. "What Logo saw! He said one of the goats had the face of a cow."

"What do you mean, Lucius?"

So Lucius explained about prodigies, and how they told about what was coming from the spirit world. He explained about the red rain and the snakes.

"You killed a rain of snakes?"

"Well, an axe did. And then, well, the Augean Stables."

When he explained about summoning the flood, her laughter rang through the caves.

"Not so loud," Lucius said. "If there is anything else in here..."

"You scold me for a troublemaker," she said, her eyes lighting up. "Just like in Rome." And she put her head against his shoulders and laughed again.

Lucius supposed she would have kissed him-- or maybe he her-- if they stayed there in the dark like that, but shy as he had become, he leaned down, touched the *baculum*, and saw that it was cool again.

"Let's go," he said, standing up. The *baculum* felt a bit chipped and flaky, but the hinge was in working condition. The cane was about half full of grammarstones now, and would need to be reloaded.

"Here," said Lucius, and put his arm behind her back, holding her hip. With a grammar on his lips, he lifted them out of the cave on the wind, and lit next to Logo, *incolumees*, who was sitting on a rock in the near-darkness.

"This is terrible," Logo said. "You are both filthy."

"Demetria was brave beyond measure," said Lucius.

"As if I have the power to tell you to do anything now,"

Logo said.

They walked back to the hut, where Kaneesh met them. Lucius let Demetria wash off in the water curtain, then went himself. Logo made a fire, and made a hot drink of wine, honey, and herbs. He asked Lucius nothing about the battle, but made a salve for his cuts from oil and herbs, and shared a few pieces of leftover flatbread between them.

"Where shall I sleep?" Demetria asked after she had warmed herself at the fire and sipped the drink.

"Here," said Logo. "And Lucius shall sleep in the cave. There is a bed there. It is quite comfortable."

"In Glyph's bed?" Lucius said.

"You will have to share it with Kaneesh," said Logo. "She is the real queen of this place."

"But it is his bed. No one should sleep in it but him."

"You are the priest of Numa Pompilius now, master," said Logo. "You are the guardian of the scrolls. And of Rome."

Master. Lucius let that word roll about in his head for a moment. He didn't feel like a master, but it was true that he had just defeated a giant. Maybe he was a master. He had done more with the grammarstones that day than in almost all his time learning about them.

Logo showed Lucius the chamber where Glyph had slept. They entered the scroll room, and went up stairs to a natural opening in the rock. The oil lamp Logo brought lit up a low-ceilinged room-- you could not stand up straight in it. There was only a bed there, and a small table for an oil lamp. The walls were covered in writing.

"It is not damp," said Logo. "It is away from the waterfall. There is even a window." He moved to the far end of the room and set the lamp underneath a hole that looked as if it had been carved and squared off.

"Put this in when it rains," Logo said, motioning with the lamp to a block of stone set on the floor near the window. "You will get some light in the morning to tell you it is time to rise."

"What are these?" Lucius said, tracing a finger along one of the strings of signs written on the wall.

"His own grammars, successful ones mostly," Logo said. "Others, not so successful. The grammar is intricate and has many levels; sometimes it works as planned, sometimes not. He did much work, and had so much to teach you."

"I will become a great *magus magister*," said Lucius. "I will be true to his memory."

"I know you will, and I am glad," said Logo, "for Rome's sake."

Logo left him to wrap up in his cloak on the bed, and pull over a soft blanket of goat fur. Kaneesh joined him, lying down at the end of the bed and grunting softly as she made herself comfortable.

Lucius was exhausted. He knew he would sleep. Tomorrow he would begin to see what he could do to protect Rome. He would begin to teach Demetria. They would look out for the Etruscans.

He would work very hard to be a master.

But as he fell asleep, a last prayer to his genius unfinished, he saw in his mind the glowing mirror of the *haruspica*, and knew he would not be a master until he had avenged his own master's death.

::XVI::

Dreams hovered over Lucius all night long.

Most of them had to do with words, signs, and letters, jumping off the wall, being spoken by ghostly voices, walking on bronze feet like the warrior he and Demetria had defeated.

None of the dreams sat down before his eyes and stayed, except for one.

He dreamed that he got up from his bed, took the cane, and left the cave, parting the curtain of water with a gesture.

He dreamed that he walked by the hut of Logophilus and saw him and Demetria sleeping peacefully, bathed in moonlight. He seemed to rise up then, above the vegetable patch, over the trees, and flew swiftly to Portentia, and to the village cemetery, where Glyph was buried. He stood and waited for Glyph's spirit to rise and speak with him, for he had been taught that one's ancestor spirits live somewhere beneath the earth, and are never far away.

But Glyph's spirit did not rise, and as Lucius stood there, he began to feel cold. A terrible grief washed over him, a sense of despair, and of wanting to go away. He thought of the Tiber River, the depth and darkness of it, and wondered if it were better to simply cast himself in and sink like a rock.

"Then I will be with Glyph," he said.

"It is not deep enough now," said a voice behind him.

He turned. A woman, or a goddess, stood before him. She looked a bit like Callidia, the servant girl, or the way Callidia might look when older, married, and a mother.

"Who are you?" Lucius wanted to say, but his lips seemed to be numb.

"Let go your anger," she said, and for a moment, her face seemed to change to Glyph's.

That was all. She faded from his sight, as into a mist, and he felt cold again. Waking, he realized that he had kicked off his coverlet. The window let in a tiny square of moonlight. He tried to rise, but fell back down, his body heavy with sleep and exhaustion.

"Even in sleep I must work," he mumbled as his eyes shut fast.

No more dreams came to Lucius that night, and he woke long after the sun rose. The mid-morning light from the window shone on his face.

"Kaneesh?" Lucius said, sitting up in bed. The dog was gone, having left only a dog-sized imprint in the covers.

He got out of bed, dressed, left the cave, and splashed his face in the curtain of water. The cane in his hands as he walked up to Logo's hut, he saw through the trees that the sun was halfway up in the sky, but clouds also were gathering to the west. It was not yet the season of storms, but they would come soon.

Lucius found Demetria and Logo at the cooking fire, seasoning tripods and cooking pans with olive oil. Seeing them working like that, a secret hope came up in Lucius' heart, that they would always be able to stay here, that no more prodigies would come, that the Etruscans would fade away as the goddess had in the dream.

"*Salve!*" Lucius called. "Greetings!"

"*Salve et tu!* Greetings to you, too," said Demetria, standing up. Her face was smudged with ash from wiping her face with dirty oil. "Don't tell me you just got up? Or have you been studying the signs this morning?"

"I wish I could say I have," said Lucius. "But instead I went flying in my sleep to see Glyph."

"Oh?" said Logo.

"I didn't see him. But I saw someone there, in the cemetery of Portentia. I think a goddess. Her name was--" and he cast about in his mind for the name that was not quite familiar to him.

"--Egeria?" Logo prompted.

"I do not remember."

"Then it was likely Egeria," Logo said. "Egeria is the goddess who first appeared to Numa Pompilius. She also appeared to all the priests of Numa thereafter, including Glyph. What did she say?"

"*Let go your anger*," said Lucius. "I do remember that. She didn't look like a goddess should look to me."

"And how should a goddess look?" Demetria said. "Something like me?"

Lucius grinned at her; Logo rolled his eyes. He said, out of the corner of his mouth, "I think it is worth saying again to you, master-- a priest of Numa never marries."

Lucius blushed, and scratched at the back of his neck.

Demetria said, "Or perhaps he marries the goddess? The lady of his dreams?" She giggled, and Lucius had a hard time not doing so as well.

Logo said, "It is important not to trifle. We are now fighting a monster with two heads. On the one hand, the *magus magister*, to whom you gave several more grammarstones, I don't wonder." He motioned to the cane which, Lucius knew, held only half a load. "On the other, we have the Etruscans. Our only advantage against them now is hiddenness, and they are bound to find us out before long. What we need is news, from Portentia, about what they are doing now."

"I think, if we meet them again, I can defeat them," Lucius said. "If we attack first--"

"First? First? Have you learned nothing?" Logo's words stabbed hard. It was the first time Lucius had seen him come close to losing his temper. "Look what happened the last time you went first."

"This is different. I know more now."

"Than you did a day ago?"

"A battle ago. We didn't tell you. I threw the *baculum*. It destroyed the demon's mirror."

Now Logo had to be filled in on all the details of the battle, and was astonished to hear of Lucius' tactic of throwing the cane like a spear.

"That was dangerous," Logo said. "It could have shattered. It could have gotten into the *magus magister*'s hands. Never let it go, Lucius."

"But I've proved that a mirror cannot stop it. I don't need

to throw grammarstones at the Etruscans."

"But once it is gone from your hand, it is gone."

"I can get it back devising a grammar."

Logo said, "It is time that you learned further. I hope I can find this scroll, so help me Egeria."

After a quick breakfast, they went down to the scroll room, and Logo unrolled a scroll that Lucius had never seen before.

"This is a scroll containing the kinds and possibilities of special words in our language. We call them *neithers*. All words in Latin are either male, or female, or neither. The male and female words are easier to use, because they are like us in a way."

"This is true in Greek as well," said Demetria. "I learned this."

"That is why it was easy for me as a Greek to understand when Glyph spoke of it in Latin. *Terra*, earth, is female. *Ventus*, wind, is male. *Baculum*--" and he pointed to the cane-- "is neither."

Lucius said, "I know that there are male and female names. My name, Lucius, is for a boy. My mother is named Junia. Demetria is a girl name, too. So is my cousin Lucretia. The king's Roman name is Tarquinius, a boy's name."

"Yes, but that's just the beginning. Everything has a nature: male, female or neither, and not every word ends in -a or -us. The most important thing to remember about the neithers is that it doesn't matter whether you name it or strike it, the ending is the same. *Baculum* is this type of word. It is *baculum* if you name it, and *baculum* if you strike it."

Lucius looked down at the signs. "It is not like *ventus*-- because the striker is--"

"--*ventom*, yes," Logo said, emphasizing the "mmm" sound at the end of the word. "And it is not like *terra*, for the striker of that is--"

"--*terrammmmm*," said Demetria, making it sound like she was just about to eat a flatbread with oil and honey.

Lucius said, "That is strange. How does one know the difference between a namer and a striker, then?"

"The other words in the grammar shape it. If there is another namer, then of course the neither is a striker. If there is no other namer, then the neither is a namer."

Demetria put up her hand. "Now you have gone too far for me."

"It is still Latin," said Lucius. "I have used neithers before in everyday speech. And it is true, if someone doesn't understand how you mean to use a neither, you simply add words until they do."

"Which makes using them in battle more difficult," said Logo. "It may be an easy thing to make the *baculum* leap back into your hand on the wind. But if you begin to use it as a weapon, and you attempt grammars that are more complex, you are liable to make a mistake."

This is what the scroll said:

	Second	Third	Fourth
Namer	vinum	aes	cornu
Striker	vinum	aes	cornu

"What's more," said Logo, "if you look at these words in the plural, the endings that indicate more than one, you see something rather strange."

	Second	Third	Fourth
Namer	vina	aera	cornua
Striker	vina	aera	cornua

Lucius said, "They all end in -a, like the female namer."

"That's what happens in Greek as well, with some words," said Demetria.

"So you must be careful to know what is male, female, and neither. The grammar does not do it for you. You must devise it."

Lucius had nothing to say. He was starting at all the letter A's on that part of the scroll.

Logo smoothed out the scroll. "By the gods, it's best not to use neithers at all. Only when there is no other word in mind."

"I only need to kill one of those *haruspices*," said Lucius after Logo rolled up the scroll. "The one who killed Logo. The others will flee when they see my power."

"You only need to make one mistake," said Logo. "And then you and I, and Demetria will all three be lost, and our spirits will join Glyph's under the earth. And what's more, there will be no one to contain the prodigies. And Rome will be lost, and with it, perhaps the whole world."

Lucius set his mouth. He didn't like to be wrong. He wasn't often wrong with his friends in Rome, and he had learned so well so far. Just one mistake-- but that mistake had taken Glyph from him. Part of him wanted to tell Logophilus not to worry, there would be no mistake. And part of him wanted to give Logophilus the *baculum*, and with it the responsibility for the world.

Logo's words had sobered them all. Demetria's grin was gone, along with her banter. It felt cold in the cave. Lucius was grateful when they went back out of the scroll room and into the light. Clouds were traveling over them now, and it was warm when the sun broke through, but the fresh breeze bit when it was behind clouds.

"I don't have time to learn more, Logo," said Lucius finally. "Maybe even today the *haruspices* will come for us."

"Remember what Glyph said. They will wait for you to move. They will wait for you to get impatient. They will learn what is in your heart, and they will use it against you."

"That sounds as if we should stay put here for the time being," said Demetria.

"Unless you would like to go home--" Logo began, then stopped. He looked Demetria up and down.

"What is it?" she said.

"I said we need news. These Etruscans have never met you before, is that not true?"

"I am just a humble Greek girl who spends all her time indoors, spinning wool."

"Then you might be of help."

"To do what?"

"To go into Portentia. As a traveling Greek stranger."

This brightened all three of them.

"I'll go with her," said Lucius, taking her hand. "I can be in disguise as well."

Demetria said, "Lucius, they know you."

"That's right," said Logo. "If they capture you, Lucius, they will make you look in their mirror, and all our secrets will be known."

"So if I fail, they will know you two are here."

"And worse. If you look into the mirror too long, your spirit will be captured inside. And that will be the end of Demetria."

"Ugh!" said Demetria. "How awful!"

"Do you still want to go?"

Demetria glanced at Lucius, who tensed up. "I can't--"

Lucius sighed and let his palms go up. "Good, it is better that you not risk--"

"--Not say yes," Demetria said. "If it will help us."

"It will," said Logo. "I promise it."

"Demetria!" Lucius said. "You are making trouble again-- for yourself."

"I do not deny it," she whispered, with a grin.

::XVII::

Demetria, the daughter of Istocles and Eodice, headed down the secret path to Portentia.

She had not seen this path when she was first seeking out Lucius. Almost no one did. That was because Portentia was the place of prodigies. That is what its name meant. And it was important that the secret be kept, for the sake of all in Rome.

For many years the Romans had been able to keep it a secret from the Etruscans, but the *haruspices* were very good at finding out secrets.

"Strangers in Portentia are rare, but expected," Logo explained. "The villagers know that a certain number come because some god has perhaps led them there. Or perhaps the visitor is a god in disguise. Many things happen in Portentia that happen nowhere else."

Demetria's story would be simple. "He" would be Antheodorus, the young assistant of a Greek cloth merchant on his way up the coast from the Greek colony of Neapolis in the south. "He" had been captured by pirates who landed at

Antium, south of Rome, and took him overland through the wilderness to sell as a slave among the Volscians. "He" had escaped in the night and wandered far, seeking shelter and a reunion with "his" master in Rome.

"Find out all you can," said Logo. "There is a girl, named Callidia. She knows Etruscan and overheard them talking about their plot against Lucius. Maybe she can tell you more. Avoid contact with the Etruscans themselves if you can; they see through disguises and unravel mysteries. Above all, don't look into their mirrors. That is the fastest way to be lost. At best, they will find out who you are, why you are here, and where we are hiding. At worst, your soul will be locked in the mirror forever."

Lucius shuddered. "There is no way out?"

"Not that I know," said Logo. "If Glyph were here, he--"

"I should be off," said Demetria, and shot a glance at Lucius.

"Come back in no more than--" Logo thought for a moment-- "three days. If you do not return, we have to assume you are lost."

"But if she is lost, then we must follow after her, is it not so?" said Lucius.

"No," said Logo. "We must do what Glyph commanded. Avoid the Etruscans and gather our strength."

Demetria felt as if she were covered with another layer of something besides her clothing. Though she was able to walk, swing her arms, swivel her neck, and see all about her as the first farmhouses came into view, and the first children and dogs swirled about her, her limbs were numb. She didn't know if she could speak. But as soon as the first child wrapped its

138

arms around her leg and said in little-child Latin, "Big boy, I want to wear your hat!" and jumped up, with fingers grasping, she knew she could do whatever was needed.

"I am a boy," she thought to herself. "Remember that, Antheodorus."

She came to the center of the town and the big house Logo and Lucius had described. The mother, Terentia, came from the house.

"Young man," she said.

Demetria straightened, and put out her hands, palms up, in a gesture of needing help. "Mother, I am lost," she said, in Latin, but with a thick Greek accent.

"You have hospitality here," said Terentia. "Come inside."

They went through the front room, dimly lit in the afternoon by a single oil lamp. Two beds were set up, with coverlets neatly folded on them. They made a left turn into a courtyard, where there was a sheltered porch, a beehive-shaped oven, a stack of firewood, a stone basin perched on a large bronze tripod, and a side room that turned out to be a pantry: onions and bacon hung from the ceiling, while jars of wine, olive oil and grain were embedded in the floor.

A girl with a face like a horse sat in front of the oven: Callidia. She poked at the embers inside the oven, warming herself. Demetria looked up. The clouds were even darker, pregnant with rain.

"Step to it, girl, we must make the bread before the rain comes," said Terentia. "What will our visitors have to eat if you spend all your time fooling with the fire?"

Terentia went over to a stone basin next to the oven and put began scooping wet dough from it to shape into loaves.

Each loaf was about as big as the amount of space in two hands, and three could go in the oven at a time. It was barley bread mixed with wheat.

"Are you hungry?" Terentia asked.

"Yes, mother," said Demetria, though she had had a good breakfast that morning of salted flatbread with a drizzle of oil and honey.

"Callidia, give him the first loaf that comes out of the oven," she said.

Callidia eyed Demetria as she waited for the loaf to rise and brown. Demetria could tell Callidia wanted to speak with her, and she got her wish when Terentia finished shaping the loaves and left to call the Etruscans to the meal.

"What is your tale?" Callidia asked. "I would like to hear it before the others do."

"Can you keep a secret?" Demetria said.

"Of course, by Castor," said Callidia.

"I come from Lucius," Demetria whispered. "To find news about the Etruscans."

Callidia gasped. "I am worried about him! Is he all right?"

"Yes," said Demetria, and raised an eyebrow. Logo had said nothing about Callidia being concerned with Lucius' welfare.

"He is a handsome young man, is he not? He left in the night with his Greek friend-- that is not one of your kinsmen, is it? And the Sage with whom he lived is dead-- stabbed with a knife. We buried him yesterday. The Etruscans said that Lucius was the one who did it, and he fled when they found him out. My uncle, Terentius, is speaking even now with them on how he might find Lucius and punish him for his crime."

"Lucius did not kill his master!" Demetria said, and Callidia jumped.

"What a boy you are, so strange! How do you know this? Lucius was so sweet to me, I could never see him doing such a terrible thing."

"So sweet to you?"

"Why, yes, we talked for a long time the other night when Logophilus sang and we had the dancers. I thought he might be keen on marrying me, he stared at me so."

"He is promised to another," said Demetria with a little cough at the back of her throat.

"Is he, then? I should not think so, I will tell you, by the way we spoke so secretly." She handed Demetria a hot barley loaf in a cloth.

"Did you kiss him?"

Callidia laughed. "It is as if you are jealous! What a thing. We might have, but I was so concerned about his life, I told him the Etruscans were plotting to kill him, and he went pale and left me. That night, the Sage was killed." She motioned to the loaf, which was still hot in Demetria's hands. "Eat, if you are hungry. It is blessed. There are more prayers in this house that nothing could ever be cursed, so I think!" and she laughed, a horse snort that made Demetria want to laugh too. Callidia might have been a friend of hers in Rome-- if she understood that Lucius was off limits to her.

Terentia came back, and instructed Demetria to sit at table in the large room in front where the beds were set up. "We will not eat outside today," she said to Callidia. "Jupiter is about to rain. Go, Callidia, to the householder and tell him to make sure the cistern spouts are unclogged. It has been months since the god visited us."

Demetria sat in a low wicker-back chair, and soon the Etruscans came-- a female and two males, as Logo and Lucius had said. She recognized one of the men, Repsuna, as a consultant for her father. He would come around when their family was sacrificing a goat to a god for a holiday, and inspect the goat's liver. The markings on the liver would tell the *haruspex* whether it was a good time to make a sea voyage or a business deal. Sometimes Repsuna would say something about the future of their family. He had predicted the birth of Demetria's youngest sister.

"The signs point to a child," he had said.

"Healthy?" Demetria's mother said.

"Yes," he said. "But ugly."

That had taken everyone aback. But Melissa, their own honeybee, had come out with a birthmark on her cheek, a dark patch that the Greeks considered lucky. No one called Melissa Melissa. Instead she had a Latin nickname, Naevia, birthmark girl.

Demetria had not taken off her *petasus* and traveling robe, and when the master of the house, Terentius, came in, he stared at Demetria but said nothing. It was not the custom among Romans to tell someone to take off a hat, and Demetria was grateful for that, because she thought the *haruspex* might recognize her.

As Terentia was putting down the bread, along with the pot of beans and bacon, she said out of the corner of her mouth to her husband, "I think it would be polite for our guest to be more comfortable."

"Let him alone," said Terentius. "He has not had a bite to eat, and we have heard no word of story from him yet."

The *haruspica*, Turanquil, tore a piece of bread from a loaf and used it to scoop beans from the steaming pot into her bowl. "We shall speak our news first," she said, "concerning the whereabouts of the murderer."

Everyone coughed or made some kind of sign to ward off the evil eye.

"Mur-der-er?" Demetria said in her thick Greek accent.

"A rash young man who could not wait to be master sage of the hills," she said. "I think whatever they do up in the hills attracted some kind of demon that his genius could not fight off."

Demetria said nothing, but bent over her dish, using bread to scoop it to her mouth. It was wonderful, savory food, seasoned with thyme and fattened with chunks of bacon.

That was all the *haruspica* said about Glyph. "We have not yet discovered where the young man is hiding, but we have spoken with the person who is in charge of supplying their grain, wine, and oil every few months. He knows more than he will say, but with your permission, Aelius Terentius Celer, we will look into his soul to discover more."

"Soul?" Demetria said. It was out before she could stop it.

"Are you a stranger to the lands of the Etruscans?" said Repsuna. "I expect you would not be, for many Greeks come and go from here."

They all looked at Demetria-- or rather, seemed to stare into her. She said, "I am... from Neapolis."

"No, you're not," said the other *haruspex*, Velthur. "A boy from Neapolis does not speak like this."

"I was not born in Neapolis," Demetria lied. "I am from..." She tried to think of somewhere else that was Greek, and instead came up with the name of the God of Everything she and Lucius had made up: Pantheos.

"Pantheos? This is a place about which I have never heard tell," said the *haruspex*. "Tell us more about it."

Against her will, Demetria began to spin a story. Logo had warned her against spending any time with the Etruscans, and now here she was, lying to them in their faces. At first she tried to make up something that sounded true, but it was difficult to think on her feet that way, so she fell back, finally, on talking about the language that she and Lucius had created.

"And there is a different tongue there," she said. "It is written on scraps of bark with a stick that has been burned in the fire."

The Etruscans leaned forward.

"The word for friend is *Arana*, and the word for hello is *Melana*. The word for goodbye is *Atana*. So when you say hello or goodbye you say *Arana Melana* or *Arana Atana*."

"It is like nothing I have heard before," said Velthur.

"How did you come to be here?" said Turanquil. She was examining Demetria with her eyes, watching her lips as she spoke, noticing the way she lifted a hand to speak.

The question gave Demetria a chance to go back to her original story about pirates. This was one she knew to tell well, because it was similar to the lie that the hero Ulysses told when he came in disguise to his own home, Ithaca, to gain information about the men who were unlawfully staying at his house.

Repsuna raised his eyebrows and said, "You are very lucky. Few escape from pirates."

"Few indeed," said Turanquil, glancing at Repsuna in a

knowing way Demetria found unsettling. "Will you now take off your hat and robe that we can see you more clearly, Antheodorus of Pantheos?"

"Ah... I would prefer not," said Demetria.

Callidia brought in apples and a hunk of goat cheese on a wooden cutting board. She kept her eyes down as she placed the dish on the table.

Turanquil said, "Girl."

Callidia stood up. She was blushing, and held herself stiff, with her hands in front of her.

"Whatever can be wrong?" said Turanquil. "Are you afraid of something?"

"Look at the guest when she speaks to you, little one," said Celer.

Callidia lifted her eyes for a moment, but then hid them again under her dark lashes.

Turanquil lifted her finger in the air, as if to shush everyone else. "Girl, do you know this boy?" she said.

"No, lady," said Callidia, gaze fastened to the floor.

Turanquil waited. Callidia lifted her face for a moment, then glanced at Demetria, who was studying the welt on an apple. Then she spoke, very quietly: "We did talk in the kitchen."

Demetria gritted her teeth. This was it. She would have to run. She would be caught. It hadn't gone well at all.

"He told me," Callidia said, and paused. "He told me he has... a birthmark on his forehead, and is ashamed of it."

Demetria jerked her head up. Turanquil *hmmmed*. Celer said, "If this is true, you ought not say it. You are shaming the guest by doing so."

"Yes, uncle," said Callidia.

A tapping sound came, which became a steady drumming: rain. Callidia went to secure everything from the kitchen, and the meal passed on to other subjects: the grape harvest, what was the best method of storing apples for the winter, how the flight of birds could predict how cold a winter it would be.

They sat at table for a long time, but Demetria, thanking the gods, did not need to speak again. Finally, Terentia came in and said they had prepared a bed for her for the afternoon nap.

"When you are refreshed, we will speak of finding an escort for you to Rome," said Celer.

Demetria learned nothing more about the hunt for Lucius, but did find out from Callidia, who came with a coverlet for the bed, that the name of the person who supplied Logo was Gnaeus.

"You need to warn him," said Demetria. "Not to say anything."

"It is not like that," said Callidia. "They will make him look in the mirror of the *haruspica*. He is lost."

"Lost?"

"His soul will pass into the mirror after they have drawn all he knows out of him. It is their way. Terentia *mater* was speaking to some other ladies, and I overheard."

"This cannot be."

"But it will happen."

"Gnaeus can't know where Lucius is. No one does."

"But they will do whatever they can to try to find him."

"Where is Gnaeus?"

"I cannot take you to see him, but ask anyone once you are out on the path. Will you tell him to flee? He will not. He knows only Portentia. He would not know to make his way

146

elsewhere."

"Thank you, Callidia," said Demetria. "You've been a big help."

"Tell Lucius I am asking my genius to watch over him."

Demetria was taken down three stone stairs to another house, through another outdoor kitchen, and into the house of one of Celer's sons. A garden plot sat between the two houses, bordered by a stick fence.

"This is the house of Primus," said Terentia. "Her wife will make you comfortable."

Primus' house was much smaller than Celer's, and there were several children here, all wide-eyed as they were herded to their parents' room for naptime, sleeping like puppies one on top of the other.

The mother motioned to a mattress set in their front room, with a goat fleece coverlet.

"The rain won't last," said Primus' wife. She was not much older than Demetria herself, perhaps nineteen or twenty. "Then next, we need to find a way to make the Etruscan weather clear out of here."

"Do you know Gnaeus?"

"I do, poor soul," she said. "He will not get a nap today, I think."

"But we need to save him, do we not?"

"What can you do against the soothsayers? And poor Glyph gone, the only one who could fight them."

"Lucius did not kill him," said Demetria. "It was the *haruspices*."

"A Greek boy from some faraway place, how do you know that?"

147

Demetria took off her hat and revealed her curls pinned up underneath it. "I am from Rome, and a friend of Lucius. We must save Gnaeus, before he tells the *haruspices* where Lucius is."

"What demon has gotten into you, Greekling?" said the wife, whispering hotly.

"Tell me where Gnaeus is."

"Won't. We're hiding him."

"I can take him to Lucius. He can hide there for now. We will find a way to destroy the Etruscans. You'll see."

"And then the whole of Tarquin's army upon us? Not a chance of it, boy-- or girl, now I see it!"

"Gnaeus will be found. Lucius will be found. There will be no one left to fight the prodigies. And then what will happen to Portentia, good lady?"

She stopped to think. And in that stopping, Demetria knew, like the good merchant's daughter she was, that she had made her sale.

Gnaeus was lying in a ditch next to a row of vines. When Demetria tapped his shoulder, he looked up, startled. His face was liked carved wood, squared off in the chin and jaw, and his eyebrows were thick, his eyes as big and grey as pebbles in a stream.

"Mercy, lady goddess," he said. "Am I on my way to my ancestors?"

"I'm not a goddess," said Demetria, though she was flattered by the comparison. "You're on your way to see Lucius and Logophilus."

"I really don't know how to get to the hut," said Gnaeus. "Truly, I don't."

"No one does, and I wouldn't either, but they are meeting me. You must come with me."

"How do we get out without being seen?"

Demetria thought. She had not taken the back way out, as Logo and Lucius had, and so all her thought was on the path by way of all those cottages.

"We'll wait for night," said Demetria.

Demetria lay on the traveler's cloak and hoped it wouldn't rain anymore. It was wet in the ditch, and there were thorns, so as they both lay there, they got wretched very quickly.

A bit before sunset, when the clouds lifted and the sun threw an orange and pink light over the fields, they began to hear people calling for Gnaeus. More than one person came by their row and pretended not to see them.

As it got dark, the whole village was lit with torches, and Gnaeus and Demetria had to pick their way through the backs of fields not to be seen. Turanquil stood in the center of the crossroads, arms across her chest. The other two were in the path out of town, also with their arms folded.

"They are patient," Demetria said.

"We will wait," said Gnaeus. "I am hungry. I hope Logophilus will have dinner waiting for us."

It became deadly silent. Even night birds did not sing. Only the torches hissed, like the tense whispers of the people.

Midnight came, and though it was not that chilly, spending the afternoon in the ditch took its toll. Gnaeus finally sneezed.

The torches moved toward them.

"Mercy, gods," Gnaeus whispered. "By my genius."

"We must run," said Demetria.

They stood up and ran along the side of the field where

they had been hiding in weeds. The torches flared as they moved in the hands of the villagers. Yet they were faster, they were closer to the path than the villagers. The only two in their way were the *haruspices*.

They held up their mirrors, but did not try to stop the fleeing youths.

"Don't look in the mirror!" Demetria shouted as they came closer.

Then, in an instant, they were running straight into the arms of Turanquil.

"There, now," she said, and caught both of them on each arm. She seemed larger than she had, and stronger.

"What?" cried Demetria. She looked behind her. The *haruspices* still held their mirrors up. In the reflection, torches, the path to Turanquil.

"The mirrors turned us," Gnaeus gasped, out of breath.

"A mirror," said Turanquil, "makes everything turn back."

A man caught Demetria away from Turanquil as she bent Gnaeus down to his knees, powerfully grasping his arm. She took out her mirror. "Now look," she said, "and tell."

Gnaeus tried not to, screwing his eyes shut tightly, but she cruelly twisted his arm, and his eyes popped open from the pain.

Immediately he went limp, and Turanquil let him go. "Now you, Greek boy who is really a girl. You are Lucius' friend, are you not? Who played with him many a day making a secret language? The signs would've told me quickly, but Velthur recognized you, and you told me the rest. Pantheos indeed."

Demetria twisted her face away. There wasn't much she could do, but at least she would do this, for as long as she could.

It almost worked. Turanquil came to grasp her hair with her left hand, and dropped the mirror. The man holding Demetria looked down at it, and screamed. He fell and let go of Demetria, who broke free, her traveling cloak ripping in Turanquil's hand.

But the other two *haruspices* had come near, and they flashed their mirrors at her so that she had to turn and hide her face. She felt Turanquil grasp her again, felt her hot breath on the back of her neck.

"Troublemaking child," she said. "Look."

Then there was a flash, and a bang, and Demetria went flying. She hit the ground and cut her face on a pebble, and had the wind knocked out of her. Heaving up and down but getting no air, she looked up to the sky and watched sparks fly up, thinking they must be her spirit going to her ancestors.

But after a moment, her stomach calmed enough to let her lungs fill with air. She turned over and looked at where she had been. Turanquil was on the ground, unconscious, and the mirror was aflame. The other *haruspices* lay on the ground, groaning, their mirrors smoking.

And Demetria saw Lucius standing above them all.

::XVIII::

Demetria scrambled over to Lucius and threw her arms around his neck. "You've defeated them! We won, Lucius. We won!"

Lucius did not return the embrace. He was staring at the flaming mirror of Turanquil.

"What have I done?" he said.

"You saved me," Demetria said. She pulled back from him, looking into his eyes. They looked haunted. "Lucius. Tell me. What's wrong?"

"I threw the *baculum* at her mirror," said Lucius.

"And it worked-- just like it did with the Bronze Warrior."

Lucius turned his head from the mirror, a quick flick of the neck, to take in the sight of Turanquil, who still lay unconscious. Her hands and arms were burned, her robe blackened and smoking.

Celer moved over to the *haruspica* and put his ear to her mouth. "She lives," he said.

"She lives," said Demetria. "But she cannot hurt us."

"It's not that." Lucius groaned and rolled his eyes.

"What is it?"

"The *baculum*. It hit the mirror and went in."

"Went in? Where?"

"Went in. To the other world. Just like the spirits do."

"How do you know? Did you see? All I saw was a flash. To tell you the truth, I still see spots."

Lucius stood over what was left of the mirror. Thin tongues of flame licked up from a molten pool of metal. The handle had bent back and collapsed into the circle. It looked like a letter Q.

"I have to go get it," Lucius said.

"What? You have to what?" Demetria said, pushing her hair back from her face.

"It is in the other world. I have to fetch it back."

"Maybe it is destroyed. Maybe that was why there was such a big bang."

"It is not destroyed." Lucius kept staring at the remains of the mirror.

Demetria persisted. "Even if you find it, you don't know how to get back."

"Logo said there was a way."

"Lucius, you'll be lost."

"It doesn't matter. Without the *baculum*, I can't perfect the grammar. If I can't perfect the grammar, I can't fight the prodigies. If I can't fight the prodigies..."

"Rome will be lost," Demetria whispered.

Their eyes locked.

"It will be the two of us," she said.

He didn't answer. He walked over to Repsuna, whose

mirror was unharmed.

"Show me," he said.

"Show me as well," said Demetria, catching up to him.

"Look in the mirror together, then, if you wish to be united forever in a living death," said Repsuna, his eyes darting away toward the field, as if he was guarding something.

They stood together and linked arms, their faces framed in the oval of the mirror. For a moment it was as if two young Romans stared out at them from another world, two young Romans like them: their geniuses.

There was another flash. Then, darkness.

::XIX::

The first thing Lucius saw was gray.

He was lying on the ground. He knew that because he felt the ground on his back, and on the heels of his feet. The soil was pebbly, gritty, and without anything growing in it.

The gray, then, was the sky.

Lucius sat up. He was in a desert, a flat, featureless plain. The ground below was the color of rust, and there were rust-colored hills in the distance. There was no wind, no sound, and there were no smells in particular except the sour grit smell of the earth.

Lucius picked himself up and dusted himself off. He was dressed as he would be while in his own world: tunic and leggings, sandals. Here, he still somehow had a body. He wasn't a breath of wind, as his people believed everyone became after death.

This must not be death, he thought.

As he turned and took in his surroundings, he marveled that he could see miles in every direction. But there was not much to see: only the flat, brownish-red plain, and the hills in the distance.

There was no Demetria, and no *baculum*.

Which way to go? It didn't seem to matter. There was no sun to show what time of day it was. It was neither hot nor cold; the air was still. The hills ringing the desert seemed to be equally distant from him.

So Lucius began to walk.

He walked for some time-- he knew not how much-- but seemed to go nowhere. The hills stayed a thin, irregular line near the horizon, somewhat darker than the color of the desert soil. Lucius began to wonder about food and shelter, though it didn't seem in this gray and brown world that any would be needed.

"Salve? Aliquis adest?" *Hello? Is anyone there?*

It was the first thing he had said aloud. The sound seemed to die as soon as it left his mouth, as if it had been spoken into a door or window that suddenly shut.

"SALVE!" The shout faded into nothing. No echo.

Not a breath of wind.

For the first time, Lucius began to be afraid. A ball of fear surrounded his heart and radiated out to his limbs. He held himself, shook his head, and dropped to his knees.

"O vente!" he cried to the gray sky, desperate for anything besides his own hands that could touch his skin.

Immediately a breeze came up. It whipped against the sleeve of his tunic. It blew a wave of dirt against his face. It whistled, and sighed.

Lucius had his eyes tightly shut. Now he opened them, and saw, all along the surface of the desert, little tornados of sand

and dirt. He was grateful for the movement, and for a second thought about nothing but took in the sight, and his heart calmed. He stood up, and felt the breeze against his face.

Now he heard something else, a moaning. At first he thought it might be the wind, but when he turned he realized that someone was kneeling almost beside him, head down, holding himself as Lucius had. He rocked back and forth on his heels, and moaned as constantly as his breath allowed it.

"Who are you?" Lucius said. The sound of his voice now traveled, though it was not as loud as if there had been no wind.

"Ohhhhhhhh," moaned the person. He was a man, young, perhaps a few years older than Lucius, and dressed as a Roman.

"It's all right, I'm here," said Lucius, and knelt down. He put his hand on the man's shoulder.

The man startled, and screamed, shying away from the contact. He threw himself face down on the ground, and pushed his face into it. He shook his head violently, and scrabbled at the dirt with his hands and feet.

"I see," Lucius said. He had seen the man's face, just for a second, and placed it. It was the face of the young man who had been made to look in the mirror just before Lucius decided to perfect the grammar of throwing the *baculum*.

Baculum speculum had been the grammar he'd devised. The cane against the mirror. It was all he could think of at the time. He'd had to leave the *casula* late. Logo had wanted to talk. He had many fears and was trying to think of plans if Demetria did not return. He was against Lucius going, even in secret, so it was already dark when Lucius excused himself to the cave, and sneaked away.

The dark had been helpful, once he was near the village. He came in unseen, extinguishing the grammarstone light he'd used to stay on the path getting into Portentia. He stayed hidden and overheard a few things from passersby, nothing helpful; finally, he crouched behind a stone wall Celer's house, where the villagers and *haruspices* stood with their torches. He knew nothing of Demetria's whereabouts until he heard a commotion near the edge of town-- cries, shouts-- and followed the crowd at a distance as they moved toward the sound.

He watched as the *haruspices* corralled Demetria and the young man who was now lying face down in this other world. Turanquil had made the young man look into the mirror, and he had fallen unconscious. She was about to make Demetria do the same thing.

There was no time to do something clever, no time to think out a grammar that would be perfect for the situation. Maybe Glyph would've been able to do it; he'd had so many years of practice. But Lucius did the first thing he thought of that made any sense at all.

Baculum speculum. The cane against the mirror. And he'd thrown the cane like a spear straight at the weapon that was going to take Demetria's life.

But now, as he watched this young man so afraid he could not abide the touch of another's hand, he realized that his grammar had gone awry.

It had gone awry because of the neithers.

Both *baculum* and *speculum* were neithers. That meant that the endings of their Namers and their Strikers were the same:

158

um, almost the sound of the young man's moaning.

Logo had said, and Lucius knew, that you couldn't tell which was the namer and which the striker unless you put more words into the sentence to make it clearer.

But Lucius, in his haste to get the grammar out, had used only two words.

So what did the grammar mean? *The cane against the mirror*, or *The mirror against the cane*? Had he unwittingly used the mirror to destroy the cane? Certainly the mirror had been destroyed; it was a molten ruin.

If only Glyph were there, or even Logo, to talk it out, explain, teach.

The wind threw another bout of grit into his face, and impatiently, Lucius said, *Nullus ventus*. Let there be no wind.

Immediately the wind stopped, and the moaning of the person on the ground became the only sound.

Lucius knelt next to the man and said, "*spes iuvenei Portentianei manu*." *Let there be hope for the man from Portentia by my hand*. And he laid his hand on the man's ankle.

This time the man did not startle, and stopped moaning. He did not get up, but sighed, and lifted his head.

"Who are you?" Lucius said.

"Gn-- Gn-- Gnaeus," he answered. "Gnaeus. Gnaeus." It was as if he were trying to tell himself so that he would remember.

"I am Lucius. Have courage. I will lead you back to your home."

"No," said Gnaeus. "No life. Death."

"There will be life. There will be."

"How?"

How? It was a good question. Lucius thought for a moment, then he straightened up, and said, "*Baculum mani magi magistri Romani ventod.*"

Cane in the hand of the Roman master of grammar, by wind.

A breeze came up again, a speck appeared out of the horizon, and rapidly got larger until it took on the shape of a cane. Lucius put up his hand. The *baculum* flew at him and he caught it out of the air.

"What?" Gnaeus said, his eyes wide.

"I have the *baculum*," Lucius said. "We will go home now."

There was still the small matter of finding Demetria, and finding a way back home as well. But it was clear that this place, wherever it was, was full of the power that Logo and Glyph had hewed out of the quarry in the form of grammarstones. There was no way his grammar would have had any effect at all without the *baculum* except if there was something like grammarstone in that place to help it have an effect.

If Lucius could perfect grammars without the *baculum*, what could he do with it?

"*Lapis viam domum ostendens*," Lucius said, *the stone showing the way home*, and threw a grammarstone into the sky. It arced up and fell on the ground. In its place, a stone path, about six feet wide, appeared and stretched off into the distance.

Gnaeus sat up, blinked, and rubbed his eyes. "You are a great sage," he said.

Lucius thought for a second that he probably wasn't quite a great sage yet, but he was proud of what he had done, so he smiled, and threw out his hand with a flourish. "Never fear. Here is the way."

He helped Gnaeus up, and dusted him off. Gnaeus said, "You are so young. You are not even half as old as the sage we buried!"

Lucius did not reply, and Gnaeus seemed to be satisfied with what he had said, so they set off on the path without continuing the conversation, and Lucius began to devise a grammar that might help locate Demetria. They had looked in the mirror together, and so he thought she would be with him in this world, but there must be something else at work.

"*Graeca viai incolums ventod,*" he said, *the Greek girl on the path unharmed, by wind.* A breeze came up, and Lucius strained his eyes to see his friend lifted on the wind toward him, crying with glee at the unusual ride.

It was as he thought, except for the crying with glee. She appeared, as had the *baculum,* her curls flying about, and then she was there, and her great black eyes looked into his.

"It is I, Demetria," she said.

"Yes, I can see that," said Lucius. "Where were you?"

"I came at your bidding. Do you not see me, do you not see that I came?"

"Of course, but where were you? How did we get separated when we looked into the mirror?"

"What does that matter? You must look ahead now. You have the *baculum* in your hands, and you have me. You will be the greatest man who ever lived."

Lucius felt a chill. He remembered when Demetria said that before, in the cavern when they fought the warrior with the mirror-shields.

"You don't have to say that," said Lucius. "Come on, it's just me."

"But you will be," said Demetria. "The greatest man."

The greatest man. It had felt wonderful to hear that from Demetria when she said it before. But now it felt strange. She was acting strangely, as if coming into this mirror-world had changed her. Could that be? He himself did not feel any different, except that all his grammars were working, everything he wanted he could do.

Maybe she had simply accepted that he was a great *magus magister*, that they were no longer friends, but he was a master, and she his handmaid.

Gnaeus said, "We still have to find a way back, as you said, young master."

Master. That word again. *Magister. Magus magister?* Could he think of himself that way now?

"Let's go, Demetria," said Lucius. "Gnaeus is right. We haven't found the way back yet. But never fear; I won't leave you again. I won't let it happen."

Demetria bowed her head, as if to say, "As you wish," and Lucius felt even stranger.

They walked for some time, no telling how long, and the hills began to appear closer. They were clifflike, resembling somewhat the wall of rock in the quarry. These hills, however, like everything on this earth, were colored rust-brown rather than gray-silver.

When they finally arrived at the foot of the hills, the path stopped abruptly in front of a cliff. There was no way of climbing up the cliff, and no portal in the wall itself where the door ended.

Lucius felt along the rough, naturally squared-off ribbons of stone in the wall. The familiar buzz of power was there. What

162

if the cave back to the quarry was right on the other side of this rock wall?

"*Lapis portam faciens*," he said, *The stone making a doorway*, and he stepped back and threw a grammarstone.

The stone hit the rock. There was a flash, an explosion, and both Lucius and Gnaeus were knocked off their feet. But when the smoke cleared, a triangular portal had appeared, going into the rock, into darkness.

Gnaeus said, "We're not going in there, are we?"

"I think we must," said Lucius.

"I don't like it. I don't want to go."

Lucius looked back at Demetria, to see what she thought. Normally, she would have an opinion about everything. In fact, they would not have walked so long in silence with the Demetria of the Roman world.

"What do you think?" Lucius said.

Demetria said, "Let this one go into the cave. It is enough for us to be together. Do you not love me, my darling? You know, that if we do go back to our own world, you cannot marry me. You are Roman, and I am Greek. My father would not consent to the match, and your father and mother would want you to marry a princess of Rome. Let us stay here, Lucius. You can make whatever you wish with your power. You can make a great kingdom out of this place. And we will be together, always."

Demetria walked up to him, looking him in the eye. She looked much older then; much more like a woman than a girl. She closed her eyes and put up her mouth to his, clasping her hands around the back of his neck.

"Beware, master, something else comes from the sky!"

yelled Gnaeus.

"Whatever it is, let it take care of itself," said Lucius, twining his arms around Demetria's waist. He felt a great sense of certainty come up in his heart, that what she had said was true. Maybe the gods had meant them to be together, here. They had come together into the mirror. Maybe they were not meant to come out.

A wind ruffled Demetria's curls. Lucius pulled her to his side. But somehow she didn't feel right. The weight of her wasn't right. Nothing was right.

::XX::

Demetria woke to darkness.

It was the kind of darkness that meant she was inside something. There was no wind, no air moving. She was lying on something-- rock, she thought, but when she sat up, and felt with her hands, and knew that "up" would be to where she lifted her chin to-- she still saw nothing, no sky, no stars, no moon, nothing.

The darkness was purest black, and thick, like fabric.

"Lucius?" she tried. They had been together a moment ago. They had looked in the mirror together. Shouldn't they be together?

Immediately there was some kind of movement, a whispering, a sighing, and a pacing of sandaled feet. Demetria had not been frightened before, but now her imagination began to work. What was there with her in the dark?

"What's there?" she said, louder, and noticed that her voice carried a long way. She must be in a large cavern with a high ceiling.

The same indefinite sounds of movement, not right next to her, but somewhere in the distance, maybe along the walls of the cavern. Nothing had touched her yet, so maybe it was not dangerous, whatever it was.

She stood up, bolder. "Go away and tell your master I must find Lucius," she said.

The sounds moved off, faded, died.

Presently a spot of light appeared, a long way off, intermittent. As she tracked the light, Demetria understood that it was going along a pathway, and that the pathway wound behind rock, so that sometimes the spot was visible, and other times not.

Soon, the light came fully into view. It was an oil lamp, and held by a young woman: a young woman who looked exactly like Demetria.

Demetria couldn't speak for a moment, as the girl held the oil lamp up, flickering, her expression neither of gladness nor pain, neither of curiosity, nor of sleepiness, but of simple existence.

Finally Demetria managed to whisper "Who are you?", her own words chilling her from head to toe.

"I am Demetria," said the girl. "I am the one who lives in the mirror."

Demetria's mouth dropped open.

"Follow me," said mirror-Demetria.

"What was it that summoned you?" Demetria said as they walked.

"Nothing summoned me," said the mirror-Demetria.

"But I was with something in the cavern, something that moved," said Demetria.

Mirror-Demetria said nothing.

They walked a long time, in total silence, until they came to a room with a large, circular pool in it. The pool looked like it held water, but as Demetria came closer, she saw that it was metal-- bronze.

"Look," said Mirror-Demetria.

Demetria leaned over, seeing nothing at first, but then she realized that she was looking at the fold of a cloak-- it was dim, but unmistakably there were the threads of a garment.

"It's-- out of the mirror that--"

"You looked at to come here, yes," said Mirror-Demetria. "It is the mirror of the Etruscan."

"Can I go back? Can I go back out of the mirror and back to my world?" Demetria asked.

"No," said Mirror-Demetria. "You are here now. You cannot go back."

"That is all? Forever?"

"Not forever. If you wish, your body will die. Then you will leave with me, I will guide you to your ancestors."

"What will happen to you?"

"I am not you. You are you." That same, even, neither-happy-neither-sad voice.

"Well, then, where is Lucius? I said to whatever was in the cavern with me that I needed to find Lucius."

"There is no Lucius," said Mirror-Demetria. "There is only Demetria."

Demetria thought hard. This wasn't supposed to have happened. Lucius and she looked at the mirror together, so they should have been in the mirror world together. But maybe Lucius was in his own cavern, with his own twin. Maybe there was no way to meet each other, as this one said. They had done what they had done with no certainty either way.

"If you wish, you may go to your ancestors now," said Mirror-Demetria. "It is your will that keeps you alive, your will alone."

"I do not wish to go to my ancestors," said Demetria. "I wish to find Lucius."

"There is no--"

"Lucius, yes, I know, you said that." Demetria looked back at the mirror pool, at the threads of the soothsayer's cloak. He had put away the mirror, was not using it; he may have been sleeping at the bedside of the *haruspica*, as they attempted to nurse her back to health. Her burns were severe.

But what was Demetria to do? What to do in this world?

"Stay here, and you will live," said the genius, answering Demetria's question without her asking it. "Or walk with me, side by side, to your ancestors."

Demetria felt a wave of heat pass over her forehead and down her back, then settle in her stomach and turn into anger. She stood up, and headed for the Demetria who had given her two intolerable choices. She pulled her hand back and slapped the double full in the face.

"I will not die!" she screamed.

Her hand passed through the genius, as if the girl-- or Demetria's hand-- wasn't there.

Twice more Demetria attempted to strike her own reflection, and twice more her hand passed through. She screamed in frustration, and the sound echoed through the chambers of her prison.

There must be something she could do.

Then she realized that the mirror pool was no longer showing the cloak of the *haruspex*.

She rushed to the pool and leaned over it. The mirror was moving. It was outside, and the light was uncertain-- either sunrise or sunset. Demetria could not see exactly where the mirror was or who had it, but after her eyes became accustomed to the light, she saw that near the corner of one side of the reflection, something like brownish-yellow fur was peeking out.

Kaneesh?

After a bit more waiting, the mirror fell on the ground, reflecting side up, and the sky came into view. There were clouds tinged with pink, and a grayish-blue sky. For just an instant, Kaneesh's face, with her little panting tongue, came into view. Then the view shifted again, and the mirror began to move, showing the path on which Kaneesh was walking.

"That's it, that's a good girl, take it to Logo," Demetria said. "He'll know what to do with it."

Kaneesh set the mirror down a couple more times, until finally, after perhaps an hour of walking, the *casula* came into view. Kaneesh dropped the mirror, and it sat in the dust for a moment until Logo's sandals and feet appeared, and the mirror rose up.

There were brief flashes of the woods around the *casula*, the garden, and Logo's cloak. He never looked directly into the shiny surface. Instead, he took it to Glyph's cave, where he set it down on Glyph's writing desk next to a number of scrolls and pieces of practice bark.

After a time, Logo left a piece of bark with signs on it-- Latin and Greek. Demetria had been taught to read a little

Greek, and she recognized the short message: DO NOT DIE. FIND *MAGUS MAGISTER. DOKANA.*

It was finished with N, the letter, the same in Greek as in Latin.

Do not die? Of course not! But what did it mean not to die? To stay there next to the pool, and wait and wait, like the reflection of a mirror, until someone else did something to free her?

What if no one could do anything? Would it not be better to die, to go off to her ancestors, to see her aunt again some day, who had told her so many stories? Would not the Underworld be a place of comfort, of family?

Demetria shuddered. *No! Anything but that!*

She looked up at Mirror-Demetria, who was looking neither at the mirror, nor at Demetria, but into some fixed point somewhere just over Demetria's shoulder.

What a ridiculous thing this genius was! With her unruly curly hair, nose too big for her face, and skin that was too brown for a respectable Greek woman. Her head and her body were not in proportion either. She often thought that she looked like a Siren from the story of Odysseus, a grotesque creature with a woman's head and a bird's body. Little, ugly bird feet.

"You are ugly," said the double, and it startled Demetria, for it had been deathly silent in the chamber for some time.

"No, I'm not," said Demetria, and stabbed at the double with an extended finger. "You're ugly. You're not me. You're trying to kill me."

"I am not you, you are you."

"By all the gods above and below, I know that!" screamed

Demetria. She felt tears on her cheeks, and impatiently rubbed her cheeks with two fingers, so that the tears went flying. "I am Demetria!" she told herself. "You are not Demetria."

More tears poured onto her cheeks, and she was going to wipe them away, but then she saw something that stabbed her in the heart.

Her double was crying, too.

She wiped at her eyes, to clear them, and walked again close to the ghostly girl that was Demetria and not. Tears fell down Demetria-genius' cheeks.

"Are you feeling sorry for me?" Demetria whispered to her.

"I do not feel, you feel," said the genius.

For the first time, Demetria understood what the genius was saying. "You are the reflection in the mirror," she said. "I am you."

"You are you," insisted Mirror-Demetria.

"You shouldn't cry," said Demetria. "It's going to be all right."

Tears continued to well up and stream down the double's face, as they did on Demetria's own cheeks.

"My aunt said this once, do you remember? Demetria, the Muses inspire the poets to tell what is hidden to ordinary people. But when they speak, they remind the poets that the poets themselves are only bellies, creatures of a day, mortal. But whom do the gods choose to give their poetry? To us. Only Bellies! Only bellies, Demetria, but receivers of beautiful words! Would the gods have given these words to bellies alone? No, my dear, we are partakers of the divine."

Demetria put her hand to her cheek, and the wet that was there set up on the tips of her fingers. She reached out to her double, her reflection, with those wet fingertips, to wipe away the tears on the ghostly cheeks.

The water on her fingers seem to bead up and to become sticky. The stickiness made a kind of ointment, an oil that touched the cheek of Mirror-Demetria and created a thread between that cheek and Demetria's finger.

"Oh," Demetria said, as all five of her fingers came close to the other's cheek and made sticky threads. Demetria leaned forward, brought her other hand, also wet with tears, to the genius' upper arm. The genius seemed to brighten for a moment, to vibrate next to Demetria's fingertips.

Then she put her own cheek next to the genius' cheek, and the tears that were there leaped out to connect them one to the other.

Finally, she extended her lips to the side of the genius' face, to the line of her jaw, and kissed it tenderly, as her aunt had with her, and as she kissed, the genius' cheek took on flesh.

Demetria felt the genius moving. It didn't move to a place, it seemed only to expand, to get bigger. Demetria cried out-- was it destroying her? Were they going to the ancestors now? If they were, it didn't matter anymore. Demetria had done what she had done.

For an agonizing moment, the genius seemed to become greater than Demetria, to meet and overwhelm Demetria, to take Demetria into herself. But then that feeling stopped. The double was not taking over Demetria. Demetria was taking over the double. Now she felt herself expanding. She was covering the double.

And then there was a third feeling, that made her tingle all over and almost want to laugh and cry at the same time: she and the genius somehow became one. It was impossible to describe, every particle of the genius and every particle of Demetria, though they should have been two, were no longer two, but one. Neither of them lost anything, but what resulted was not they together. It was Demetria, herself, whole.

Then the cavern dissolved. The dark dissolved, the feeble light of the lamp, and the light that came from the pool, all were swallowed. There was nothing there anymore. She felt she was flying. A breeze came up, and she rode it as if she were riding a horse with her feet on each of the horse's flanks. A great, rust-brown circle came into view below her, like a mirror. She was flying down to the surface of the mirror. As she came closer and closer, she realized that the edges of the mirror were hills, and the surface of it earth.

And as she got even closer, she realized that there were three figures on the ground, next to the hills, that were like cliffs. One of them was Gnaeus. One of them was Lucius. And one of them was Demetria.

And she was kissing Lucius.

::XXI::

"Wait a minute!" cried Demetria as she lit on the rust-brown earth, her sandals crunching on the pebbly ground.

Lucius let the other Demetria go.

"Not again!" Demetria said. "I've had enough of twins, enough for the rest of my life!"

The other Demetria frowned at Demetria and said, "Tell this accursed spirit to be gone, my love! It is clearly an enemy that we must defeat, as we did in the cavern with the Bronze Warrior."

Lucius, thank the gods, had the *baculum* in his hand, but Demetria's relief at the sight quickly changed to confusion when she saw him raising the *baculum* to loose a grammarstone at her.

"No, Lucius, don't!" she shouted. "I'm Demetria. That... one isn't me. There is only one me, and I am she!"

True words, if silly. But they didn't stop Lucius from chambering a grammarstone. The click chilled her utterly, and she swallowed hard. "Lucius," she said. "Lucius, don't."

174

"Destroy it, before it destroys us, darling!" said the other Demetria.

"Lucius, you can't. It's me. I'm telling you, it's me."

Lucius stared hard at her. "How do I know it's you?"

"Because it is. I'm me. Remember? Demetria. The troublemaker."

"But you are no longer a troublemaker," Lucius said. "You and I--" he hesitated, 'and blushed. "We are going to be married. You are-- she is-- we have decided."

Gnaeus then said, "Master Lucius, I think you might--"

"Quiet!" said Lucius. "I am the master. I decide."

"Lucius," said Demetria. "Lucius. You're still Lucius. Don't forget who you are."

"I am a master, I am a *magus magister*."

"You are a young man," said Demetria. "Who has been training a few months. Remember Glyph, remember Logo."

"In the cave, you said I'd be a great man."

"Darling, destroy it," said the other Demetria. "It is past time. It will gather strength if you let it live."

Lucius lifted the *baculum* and cocked his arm.

"Lucius, no," said Demetria. "You can't. We can't. We have to go back."

"I'm staying here."

"No, Lucius."

"*Lapis Graecam...*" Lucius began. *The stone against the Greek girl...*

A tear flew from Demetria's cheek as she shook her head. She lifted her palms to him, and said, "*Arana Atana.*" *Farewell, friend.*

Lucius whipped the *baculum* forward. "*Lapis Graecam falsam*

175

transfigens," he said. *The stone piercing the false Greek girl.*

Demetria shielded her face with her forearm, as if that would stop the grammarstone. But no grammarstone flew at her. Instead, Lucius let the stone fly into the air, and it came down-- bending toward the false Demetria.

The *Graeca falsa* disappeared with a deafening bang.

In her place, there was Lucius-- another Lucius. And he had a *baculum* of his own.

"More twins!" Demetria said to herself. "By all the gods! This is a crazy place."

The twin Lucius drew back his cane and let fly a stone at the real Lucius. There was no grammar, just the stone, and the real Lucius deflected it with his cane. It rattled up against the cliff wall and exploded.

Gnaeus cried out, and scrambled inside the portal.

"Get behind me!" Lucius screamed at Demetria.

"So long as you believe I'm me," she said.

"Of course," he said, and let a grammarstone go with a grammar to create smoke in front of the twin Lucius. They were swathed in opaque grey-white mist. "*Atana Melana*," he said. *Hello, friend.*

Demetria sighed. "Never do that again."

"We should retreat into the cave," said Lucius. "And escape this one. The *baculum* is dangerous and as full of stones as mine is."

"Don't run from yourself," said Demetria. "I learned that just now."

"What?"

"Don't..." she tried to find the right words. "He is not your enemy. That's all."

"What do you mean?"

But Demetria had no time to speak. A wind came up, and swept away the smoke, and there was the other Lucius, with his cane cocked and ready.

Lucius cocked his own weapon, a grammarstone rattling into the chamber.

"Shield your head and eyes, it's going to be fire this time. We'll see if it can withstand that."

"No!" Demetria said, and took hold of Lucius' arm.

The Lucius twin let another grammarstone go. They ducked, and the stone went into the portal and exploded somewhere inside the cavern. Dust and shards of stone flew at them from behind, and temporarily obscured them again.

"Don't destroy it!" Demetria said, then hit on something. "It can't speak. You know it can't. It hasn't said a word yet. It is not as powerful as you. You're the only one who can destroy yourself!"

The other Lucius let fly a grammarstone, and the real Lucius whacked it away with the cane. It went flying halfway up the cliff wall, exploded, and sent a rain of stone down on them.

"It is more powerful than I," said Lucius.

"NO, Lucius. Only you are more powerful than you." And she embraced him around his neck.

Lucius stiffened. He stood up tall, and Demetria let him go.

"Let me," he said.

He cocked the *baculum* again, and so did his twin. He wound up. He threw.

Not a stone. The *baculum* itself.

The other Lucius threw it as well.

But only one cane flew: the double's. The real Lucius had followed through, but instead of throwing the cane, brought it back down to the ground, and ducked.

Demetria and Gnaeus threw themselves to the ground as the other cane windmilled over them.

A great bang and flash and concussion of air knocked Lucius to the ground.

When the smoked cleared, the other Lucius was gone.

"Oh, thank the gods," said Demetria. "That is it. It's over." She could hardly hear herself for the roaring in her ears from all the explosions.

Lucius stood up, cane in hand. "I don't think it's over."

"What?"

Lucius pointed behind Demetria. She turned.

There, standing in the threshold of the portal, was a man who looked something like Glyph. He had a tattoo like Glyph, of concentric circles around his eye. But this one surrounded his left eye, not his right.

He was dressed in a long robe, shawl, leggings and sandals. On his fingers were several rings. And in his hands was a *baculum*.

"*Salve*," said the man, in a voice not unlike Glyph's. "I am Caius Litterarius, the one whom you call *magus magister*."

::XXII::

"Come in," said the man who looked like Glyph. "You don't want to stay out there. That is a place of insanity."

Lucius didn't move. "You don't much look like that head I saw in the vegetable garden earlier this year."

"If you knew how many grammarstones I swallowed just to get a look at you, you wouldn't mind so much. We do what we must." He motioned with the *baculum* into the threshold of the portal.

"How did you get that *baculum*?"

"You threw it, of course."

"I didn't throw it. My twin--"

"You are the only you there is," said the *magus magister*. He sounded like Glyph, but his tone was different-- mocking, superior. Glyph had never mocked him.

Demetria said, "You can't destroy us, as long as Lucius has his *baculum*."

"I don't want to destroy you, girl," said the *magus magister*. "I want to get out of these other worlds, back to where I was

179

born. That's all. And with this--" he hefted the *baculum*-- "and you, I now can."

"Come on," he said. "It's the only way back."

Gnaeus said, "He speaks reasonably, friends. Anyway, I don't want to meet my twin again."

"You met your twin?"

"Oh, yes. It's why I was so scared, young master, when you found me. It came at me like an animal and I thought it was going to tear me limb from limb. But when we rolled over and over, and fought some, then I realized it was only I. And that scared me plenty, I do tell you, young master."

The *magus magister* cocked his head, motioned inside again.

"As long as you know my *baculum* will be at the ready," said Lucius.

"I would be disappointed if it weren't," said the *magus magister*. "And I hope you will call me Caius. It is the name my father gave me."

"As you wish," said Lucius.

They walked inside, and Caius threw a grammarstone from his *baculum*, and with a grammar made light for them that hovered above their heads as they walked. The path was irregular-- sometimes straight, with gravelly soil underfoot, sometimes descending stairs, or short cliffs nearly as tall as they were. They had to climb, too, boosting themselves on outcrops of rock.

Through it all, Lucius became aware that he was neither tired, nor hungry, nor thirsty. He simply kept on going.

Caius spoke when they were not exerting themselves on climbs or descents. "We have a long way to go. The mirror world and the spirit world of Latium are connected, as is

Etruria and Rome's territory. But it is not easy to get to one from the other."

He tapped at the cave wall with the *baculum* as he walked. "We will finally find ourselves in the caverns near the quarry, where you explored, and where you both defeated my Bronze Warrior."

"Did you create that?" Demetria said.

"I did," said Caius with a smirk. "It was one of my better inventions. It took many grammarstones. All I had at the time. And I almost got the *baculum*, didn't I? How foolish of you to throw it, Lucius. It did destroy the warrior, and I hadn't the strength to pick it up before you did. But it gave me hope that someday I could have it."

They descended rough-cut stairs, and the flopping of their sandals echoed into the distance.

"We are bodies, not spirits," said Lucius. "And yet I neither hunger nor thirst."

"We are not bodies," Caius said, as if it was the truest thing he'd ever said in his life. "Our spirits tell us we are bodies, and there is enough power in the mirror world and in these caves to create something that looks and feels and sounds like bodies. But I can tell you, as someone who has not had a body in many, many years, this is a poor excuse for a body."

"So we must reunite with our bodies, outside," said Demetria. "I asked my double if I could go back through the mirror I went in by. She said no."

"No, you cannot. The mirror is a one-way portal. The way to the quarry is two ways. But you must have enough power to break through. Worlds do not connect so easily that you can go back and forth. We all know that the world of death is the hardest to break. You cannot go there and come back. No one has, or ever will."

"Hercules did," said Demetria.

"A story," said Caius.

They didn't speak for some time, and presently the light above them faded. "Lucius, use your stone this time. There are only so many in my *baculum*."

Demetria shook her head, but Lucius cocked and threw. "*Lucs antrei.*" *Light in the cavern.* "He's right. It's only fair."

"But what assurance have we that you're not leading us deeper into the caves, to kill us and take the other *baculum*? Why should we follow you?" Demetria motioned ahead of her with a hand. "This path is never-ending. Where does it go?"

"It is true that I might be able to defeat Lucius and take the cane," said Caius. "But at what cost? How many grammarstones will we lose fighting each other? Would I have enough left to get out? To get through and outside, there is need of much power, and it will be a frightful thing to rejoin our bodies. I am not foolish." He wiped sweat from his brow. "I want to get out of here. You will go with me."

"How did you get in?" Lucius said.

Caius laughed bitterly. "It is a sad story, for me. Long ago, two brothers came to be initiated into the priesthood of Numa Pompilius. Learned signs. Learned the grammar that the goddess Egeria had taught Numa. Knew that we must keep the prodigies of the other world from overwhelming ours. We always knew there could only be one true priest because there was only one cane. But we thought one of us would be master, the other a servant and companion."

"You and Glyph are brothers," Lucius said. "You have the

same family name-- Litterarius."

Caius made something like a nod, and went on. "Glyph was the more gifted, but I was the more ambitious. When the time came to bestow the *baculum*, the priest gave it to Glyph. I was beside myself with rage. I went into the caverns, looking for something I could use to counteract the *baculum*, something greater so that I could be the protector of Rome. Instead I went in too far, my spirit was separated from my body, and here you see me. I have become master of the prodigies."

Now Demetria said, "How can you get back to your body?"

"It is there, it is preserved. It will be ready when I come back."

"And then what?"

Caius didn't answer. Instead, they descended a long staircase, and at the bottom there was a level area, with a great cavern, and stalagmites and stalactites. Up to that point, Lucius had felt no temperature change. But now, it was noticeably cooler.

"We are close now," said Caius.

"Do you still want to be the priest who protects Rome?" Lucius said.

"No, you may do that, young man. The prodigies will still come. The other world wishes to break into this one."

"And you?"

Again, Caius said nothing. They made their way across the field of stalagmites, and for the first time, Lucius began to feel as if there were something familiar about his surroundings. They came to the other end of the cavern, and there was a doorway, two vertical posts of stone with a lintel topping it, like the Greek letter pi. On either side of the doorway was carved a snake, and at the top, in the middle of the lintel, a sunburst or flower. The door itself was no door, but smooth darkness.

"These are the *dokana*," said Caius. "If you go through, you will find yourself in the caverns next to the quarry. But this is as far as spirits can go without the *baculum*."

"You mean you need to hold the *baculum* to get through?"

"I do not know. I have not yet tried."

"You sound like a wise man, but even I can see this will not work," said Gnaeus. "There are two sticks, and four people."

"It is so," said Caius.

"Perhaps we can go through together, holding the *baculum*," said Demetria.

"Or maybe there is not enough power to do that," said Caius.

"Or maybe we can just walk through, and you are fooling us, master Caius," said Lucius. He advanced to the *dokana*, and put a hand into the threshold. There was something hard there, impenetrable, like stone or metal, but nothing could be seen. His fingers splayed out on it.

"You cannot go. I would have," said Caius.

"And if we throw a grammarstone at it?" said Lucius.

"Throwing a grammarstone will not help. I have used grammarstones to project my image, as in the garden. What we need is something much stronger." And he rattled his cane, less than half full with grammarstones.

Lucius checked his own cane-- there were fewer in his.

"We need a full *baculum*, and we need to cast it at the door, as you did to the mirror of the warrior. I need you to give me your cane, so that I can fill mine with grammarstones, and we can throw it at the door."

"Will that open it for all of us?" Demetria said.

"I would expect," said Caius.

"But then I would not have a *baculum* with grammarstones. You would."

"That is correct as well. But we do not know whether the *baculum* will be destroyed in making a way through the portal."

Lucius shook his head. "I don't trust you. I can't give up this power."

"Nevertheless, you must."

"Throw yours now, it will open," said Demetria to Caius.

"Not a chance of it, girl," said Caius, not even turning to her. "And leave myself without a cane, and you with one less than half full? We would be stranded forever."

"Oh, by all the gods and the god of everything," Demetria said, biting a nail.

"You give me your *baculum*," said Lucius to Caius. "I will throw."

"Don't throw it, Lucius," said Demetria. "You vowed never again to do it."

No one had any more breath for words. They stood, panting, and the light that Lucius had made bobbed up and down above them.

"There's just one thing," said Lucius presently. "I went looking for the *baculum* in the mirror world. But when I went there, only my spirit went, not my body. Isn't it true that this that I think I hold, is not a real *baculum*, but only its shape, its likeness, made to look and feel like a *baculum*? Is that why there so easily became two of them when I battled my twin?"

"Well done, young *magus*," said Caius. "The only thing real in all of this is the grammarstones."

"So all this you say about there being two canes, and I can rule the prodigies with one, and you can go on your way, and not answer us when we ask what you will do with it, this is all nothing?"

Caius leaned on his cane. "It is not nothing. I have counted twenty-six stones between us in these two spirit sticks. And I have gathered another nine during the battle with the Bronze Warrior. That makes thirty-five. The same number as the original list of kinds and possibilities. Enough."

"Where are those nine you speak of?"

"In the back of my throat," said Caius. "You saw them."

Lucius shuddered, recalling the moment.

"So where," said Demetria, "is the real *baculum*? The one Lucius threw into the mirror?"

"No doubt it is with Glyph, in his own cave. That is where my body is as well."

"What?"

"Glyph has preserved my body all this time in the caverns of Egeria," said Caius. "If he had wanted to, he could have killed me. But he did not want to kill his own brother. He has been keeping me in prison this whole time."

"Do you not know, then?" Demetria said.

"Know what?"

"That Glyph is dead," Demetria said.

Caius seemed not to react. If anything, he held his body stiller than he had before. "Then I must take my leave as quickly as possible, for the power he used to keep my body alive is waning. I must rejoin it. Give me the cane, Lucius."

"No, you won't have anything from me," Lucius said. "You

lied to me before, who says you are not lying now?"

"You are making a mistake. If we throw the *baculum*, the door will be open, and we will all be free. There will be no *baculum* in either of our hands. It is with Glyph."

"How do we know you won't immediately go to get the *baculum* and take over the power of the grammar?"

"I am too old for that kind of power."

"You're lying."

"Give the cane to me, Lucius. I know better."

"You will use the power of the *baculum* wrongly once you get it."

"I will simply take it from you, then." And Caius Litterarius stepped forward.

Lucius stepped back and raised his *baculum*. Gnaeus and Demetria flanked him.

"Do not loose a stone, there won't be enough--" Demetria began, but instead of finishing, screamed.

Caius swung his cane at Lucius, who blocked it with his. There was a smack, and a clatter, and Lucius almost dropped his cane, but he was able to ward off Caius' blow.

Again, Caius wound up and swung. Gnaeus and Demetria dodged out of the way, and Lucius took the blow straight in the middle of his cane. His hands stung, and the feeling went to his elbow. He could hardly hold on to the *baculum*.

He is strong for a spirit! Lucius thought to himself, and braced for the next blow.

This time it came from above-- Caius was taller than Lucius, and he whipped it around his shoulder fast. Lucius blocked it, but his wrist tendons were on fire, and he dropped the cane.

187

"Good," said Caius, and leaned over to pick up Lucius' *baculum*.

"You won't!" said Lucius, leaping forward and kicking his own *baculum* out of Caius' hand.

The *magus magister* whirled and swiped at Lucius' legs; Lucius jumped over the cane as it flew in a half-circle.

Both of them recovered their balance and caught their breath, and then Lucius made a try for his own cane, which had come to rest in a corner.

Caius caught up with Lucius and struck him in the shoulder. It felt to Lucius as if his whole body had been shattered. He rolled over, pain radiating through him, but realized he could still move; what's more, he was lying on top of his *baculum*.

Caius brought down his cane with both hands. Lucius rolled again, exposing his cane. The two canes met, and there was a deafening crack.

Both canes split in two, and the grammarstones spilled out.

"Yes," said Caius, and fell on top of the pile.

"What is he doing?" Demetria said.

"Swallowing them," said Lucius. "Get--"

But a stone came whistling from the other side of the room and slammed directly into Caius' head. He stiffened, then collapsed on the ground. The stone clattered on the floor.

Demetria and Lucius turned.

Gnaeus was still in his follow-through, standing on the flat surface of a nearby boulder, a rope sling trailing from his hand.

"Begging pardon of the *magus magister*," said Gnaeus. "And you, young master. But I knew this spirit sling would come in handy sometime. And I just needed a clear shot."

Demetria screamed and clapped. Lucius clasped Gnaeus' hand. Caius did not move.

"Help me gather these grammarstones," said Lucius. "Get them out of his mouth. Don't bother with the ones in his throat."

"No fear of that!" said Demetria. "Eww!"

Gnaeus said, "What are we going to do with them? Not swallow them, by the gods."

"We need to figure out how to get through the *dokana*," said Lucius, as he picked up a split portion of a *baculum*. "Without using this, of course. And Gnaeus, if you wouldn't mind keeping another stone at the ready. We don't know when spirits wake up from being brained!"

"As you wish, master," said Gnaeus, scrambling down from his perch.

"It seems to me that once you have these stones about you, you can try a grammar on the door," said Demetria. "Why not? The power is there, if you perfect the grammar."

They gathered all the stones except the ones in Caius' throat, and put them in the fold of Lucius' cloak. Then he began trying grammars:

"*Porta iuvenibus aperiens*," he said. *The gate, opening for the youths*. Nothing.

"*O vente portam iuvenibus aperiens*," *I summon the wind opening the door for the youths*.

"*O vente portam spiriteis aperiens*," *I summon the wind opening the door for the spirits*.

"Don't try with the wind anymore," Demetria said. "Don't try to summon anything. There is nothing here that's real, not the wind, not anything-- except for the grammarstones."

"You're right," said Lucius. "We must tell the door to open, but we've already done that, and it won't work."

"Maybe you do have to throw a stone at it," said Gnaeus.

"Or more than one," said Demetria.

"I don't think so," said Lucius. "Didn't Caius say this door has a special name?"

"The *dokana*," Demetria said. "It is a special word. It isn't Latin; it's Greek. Logophilus mentioned it in his message to me."

"Message?"

Demetria told the story of Kaneesh's theft of the mirror, and how Logo had used it to give them advice. They had followed it well, but now there was no more help to be gotten from it.

"Do you know anything more about this *dokana*?" Lucius asked.

"Only that my aunt once said that the divine twins, Castor and Pollux, are guardians of this gate. She spoke about it as the gate between the living and the dead."

"Maybe we must use this word instead of *porta*. It is a very special door."

Demetria and Gnaeus agreed. Lucius tried again-- and again, the door remained shut.

"We'd best be making more light, young master," said Gnaeus, "or--"

"Wait a minute," said Lucius. "Did you say that Castor and Pollux are guardians of the gate? Guardians. As in more than one?"

"Yes. As in twins. Like the reflection in a mirror, and the person."

"Then is it possible that *dokana* refers not to the door itself, but to the posts of the door? With Castor and Pollux on either side?"

"But what difference does that make?"

"All the difference in the world to the grammar!" said Lucius. "If the *dokana* is more than one, the grammar must also be more than one. It must match."

"I don't understand."

"*Porta*, gate, is singular and female. *Dokana*, gate-beams, let's call them, is plural and neither male nor female. You remember that scroll that Logo rolled out for us, and how there were endings with the letter A for words that were neither and plural."

Demetria shrugged. "In Greek, neithers have only one number. They are always singular."

"But in Latin, they are plural. Wait..." and Lucius gathered all the grammarstones in his hand, and went to the posts of the door. "Come, both of you! Help me!"

He directed them to link arms and hold grammarstones in their hands. Gnaeus stood on one end, grasping a beam, Demetria in the center, and Lucius on the other.

"Now we are truly like Castor and Pollux, with the lady Helen, their sister, in the middle!" Gnaeus cried.

"*Dokana antrei iuvenibus spiriteis* aperientia," said Lucius, *The gate posts in the cave opening for the youths who are spirits*, substituting *aperientia*, the plural, for *aperiens*, the singular.

Immediately there was a rumbling and a shaking, like an earthquake. The gateposts started to shift and come apart. The companions held on to each other as the posts separated, and Gnaeus and Lucius held to the beams.

"They will pull us apart!" Demetria screamed.

"Hold on!" cried Lucius. "Keep a hold of the grammarstones!"

It seemed to take forever, and as they held on, they were being pulled away from each other. Hands left hands, slid down fingers, fingers only held on to fingers.

The stone of the wall cracked and boomed. Pieces of rock fell from the ceiling. Dust rose from the floor.

"Please! By Hercules!" Lucius groaned.

The opening became so wide, they were pulled off the ground, their bodies pinned against the surface of the door that was so strong and yet seemed not to be there. And their arms grew taut, so that-- they if anyone could see them-- they would have made what looked like three vertical lines crossed with one horizontal.

"I cannot hold!" Gnaeus said.

"Hold!" screamed Lucius, his legs dangling.

Cracks of light appeared all around the posts, and the threshold, and the lintel. The cavern moaned with the sound of air being let in.

"Only a little more!" Lucius cried.

The light grew more intense, and began to eat the dark of the door itself. It was not opening as much as it was disappearing in the light, and the three companions were being consumed in it.

And they knew no more.

::XXIII::

"You are so impatient," Logo was saying. "If only you had waited. I could have told you."

Lucius managed a sheepish grin. He was sitting in front of the fire at the *casula*, with Demetria and Kaneesh next to him, and flatbread warming on the cooking disk. It was midday, three days after Lucius and Demetria had left the world through the Etruscan mirrors.

"You would have been trapped in the spirit world forever," Logo said.

"But grammar saved us," Lucius finished for him.

All three of them-- Lucius, Demetria, and Gnaeus-- had woken up more or less at the same time in beds in Celer's house. They had been taken there after the fight with the mirror, along with the injured *haruspices*.

"We followed your message, dear Logophilus," said Demetria. "It was so clever of Kaneesh to steal the mirror of the *haruspex*. What you wrote was clever, too. How did you know I would see the message?"

Logo straightened up at the compliment, and the scowl on his face lightened. "I didn't know you would see it. I thought perhaps. And when I wrote N--"

"Meaning *neither*," Demetria put in.

"So you figured that out as well?"

"I did, on my own," said Lucius. "She didn't tell me about the N."

Demetria stuck out her tongue at Lucius.

"And you met the *magus magister*," said Logo.

"Yes," said Lucius. "He said his name was Caius Litterarius."

"He was like Glyph," said Demetria. "But different, too."

Logo grunted a yes. "Did you speak-- or just battle and defeat him?"

"He wanted us to be his ally," said Lucius. "But he lied to us about it."

"Then I must show you something, after our meal."

They went on to tell the whole story, how they had found out Caius was Glyph's brother, about Gnaeus saving the day by hitting their spirit enemy with a spirit rock that knocked him unconscious.

"I would like to go to that spirit world someday," said Logo. "What one could learn."

"I would have thought that you would want to sit here forever at your fire, and tend the goats, and plant and pick the vegetables."

"You forget, I am a poet," said Logo. "It would be fine to tell my own story, that I had lived."

The day was brisk, the sky was covered, and rain was on the way, so it was a comfort when Logo brought them into the shelter of Egeria's caverns.

"There is one place you have not seen yet," said Logo.

They went into the scroll room, and Logo pointed at the place where Kaneesh usually emerged, having taken her shortcut from the *casula*. It was a fissure in the rock, not tall or wide enough to be a door, but by stooping, and turning to the side, one could easily get through.

They took an oil lamp with them, and as soon as they were through the fissure, a chamber opened up, larger than the scroll room, but with a lower ceiling. On a kind of natural bed lay a body, covered in blankets. Two urns, filled with grammarstones, had been placed at either side of the bed. Logo went forward, but the youths stayed back.

Logo turned to them. "Come," he said. "It is all right."

"Is it the *magus magister*?" Lucius asked.

"Yes," said Logo. "Come."

They knelt at the head of the bed. There, turned on its side, was the body of Caius Litterarius, with its tattoo on the left side of his face.

Lucius shuddered, and turned away.

"Glyph's brother," said Demetria quietly.

"Glyph kept him alive," said Lucius. "Even though he was dangerous."

"Yes," said Logo. "I suppose I must apologize for Glyph. We didn't tell you. It was a difficult thing."

"He will die some day," said Lucius. "Won't he?"

"Of course," said Logo. "Though the grammarstones preserve his body longer than a normal man's life." And he motioned to the urns.

"He will wake up," said Demetria, "and find out that we left him behind, won't he?"

"And will be angry," said Lucius.

"He can do nothing at this point. He hasn't enough grammarstones."

"But when he gathers enough," Lucius said, and turned his palms upward. "But instead, we could..." He trailed off, and put his hand to his forehead, thinking hard.

Logo fixed him in his gaze. "What are you saying?"

Lucius blinked. "Is there a way? To remove the urns? To let him-- die?"

"Lucius!" Demetria gasped.

"It was Glyph's wish that he live," said Logo. "If you are here, he cannot use the prodigies for ill."

Demetria stood between them. "But what if we bring him out? Now that we know how to get out of the *dokana*, should we not go back in through the mirror, and rescue him?"

"He is dangerous," said Lucius.

Logo said, "Lucius is right. We could never trust him. He has a lot of anger stored up in the years he has been in the spirit world."

Demetria continued to argue. "But if we brought him out, he would be grateful. He would owe us a debt he could never repay. And we would say that he must live out his days here, at the *casula*, and give up his idea of controlling the *baculum*."

"The *baculum*," said Logo. "That's the other thing. Your work is far from done, Lucius. I had Kaneesh return the mirror, but the *haruspices*--"

A sound came from Caius, something between an exhalation and a sigh.

"That happens now and then," said Logo. "It is of no--"

Another sound came. It was a word, unmistakable: "Glyph."

Then again: "My brother."

Then, "Egeria."

Another sigh, a long one.

Logo knelt down, put his ear to Caius' mouth. "He does not breathe," he said.

Demetria, full of awe, whispered, "When I was in the mirror world, my double said I could go to my ancestors with her."

Logo felt for a pulse on Caius' neck, shook his head.

Lucius said, "He has made the journey."

"He is with his brother," said Demetria.

There was a rush of wind. Immediately, the oil lamp they'd brought with them lost its flame. The wind whipped at the trio's garments, freshened, blew harder, filling their ears with a roaring. The wind became so strong it knocked over the urns, scattering grammarstones.

"In a circle," Logo screamed over the wind, and they sat and held each other, arm over shoulder.

Then the roaring grew even greater, but it was mixed with a hissing, and a ticking, as if sand or glass was being whipped up into the whirlpool of air. The blankets of the *magus magister* flew off, and the hiss became even greater. Grit flew into the air, hit Lucius' eyelids, flew up his nose. Demetria coughed violently. Logo held them closer.

Then it was over. The wind died. In the almost-darkness of the chamber, with only a sliver of light coming from the fissure in the rock, Lucius saw that the bed was now empty.

Caius Litterarius, the *magus magister*, was gone forever.

197

D.W. FRAUENFELDER

::XXIV::

They staggered outside, grateful for the fresh air, even though it had started to rain. They washed their faces in the curtain of the water, and watched the rain come down, wetting the world.

"Zeus rains," said Logo, and it was a long time before anyone spoke again.

"Jupiter," said Lucius.

"One and the same," Logo said.

"Anyway, there is only one kind of water that falls from the sky," said Demetria.

Finally, they retreated to the scroll room, lit oil lamps, and made plans.

"Only one question remains," said Lucius. "Where is the *baculum* of this world?"

"An easy one," said Logo. "It did the very same thing your body did when your soul was drawn into the mirror world. It stayed here."

"Here? Where?"

"In the field where it landed. It passed into and through the mirror-- its soul went into the mirror world and it split the mirror in two-- and it fell twenty-five paces away and lay in some grass, unnoticed."

"Why didn't we see it?" Demetria asked.

"There was a fire," said Lucius. "And smoke."

Logo bowed to Lucius. "There is that."

"Did you find it? Do you have it?" Demetria asked.

"No, alas," said Logo. "I was exhausted the night that we sent you to Portentia. If I had had better judgment, I would never have let you go. And then this one--" he pointed at Lucius-- "decided it would be a good thing quietly to follow you after I fell asleep. I did not wake till the next morning, fairly late. Kaneesh and I took her secret way into Portentia-- she has friends who feed her there, I found-- and I met Celer, who told me the whole story and how they were nursing Turanquil, who had been badly burned. The other two *haruspices*, however, recovered from their wounds and found the *baculum* soon after you used their mirrors to go the other world."

"So they have it?" Demetria pursued.

"Yes, and according to Celer, they went back to Rome as soon as Turanquil was well enough to travel by litter. You were gone three days; enough time for her to recover at least a little."

"They don't know how to use the cane, do they?"

Logo shook his head vigorously. "No, indeed, not yet. Their first language is Etruscan, but they know Latin to speak it, and although they understand nothing of the grammarstones, if they were to find this place, certainly they could study the scrolls and learn."

"But we need to get the *baculum* back to fight the prodigies," Lucius pointed out.

"There will be fewer prodigies now that Caius is gone. But there is no telling what ill could happen if the *baculum* falls into the wrong hands."

"Such as those of Tarquinius," said Lucius.

"Someone who likes to kill his enemies?" said Demetria.

"Tarquinius can do that now," said Logo. "I am speaking about whole cities, whole peoples, in a moment."

"Glyph said that was possible," Lucius said. "But I cannot do that."

"Study, and you can," said Logo. "Glyph could, but he chose not to. I am telling you, there is power in this place. One day, the power will be so great, it, and Rome, will rule the world. The question is, will it be a world with one king and only slaves and dead enemies, or will men rule it together, in the strength of hands held and hearts as one?"

"There is nothing else besides a king," Demetria said. "Is there?"

"You have grown up with a father," said Logo. "A king is all you know. But there are men who have begun to understand-- the agreement of the people ruling themselves is where justice lies. This is called a republic."

"We have that already. It is called the boy's council," said Lucius.

"And that will be, someday, a council of men, if you help make it so."

"And what about a girl's council?" said Demetria.

"Someday," said Logo. "Not now."

Demetria frowned.

Lucius asked, "Can they destroy the *baculum*, as the spirit *baculum* was destroyed?"

"No, I don't think so," said Logo. "But if the spirit *baculum* is no more, I fear for the real one. The two are linked."

"How are we going to steal it back? They will guard it, I think," said Demetria.

"I know how to get it," said Lucius. "Devise a grammar and it will fly back into my hands."

"If you are not near the quarry, you will need to be very close to the *baculum*."

"What about if I have grammarstones?"

"You need the *baculum* to make full use of the grammarstones," said Logo. "But they do have a habit of making a bang when they hit something."

"Thrown from the hand?"

"Perhaps."

"What about a sling?" Demetria said.

"A swiftly-thrown stone is better than a slow, yes."

Lucius and Demetria turned to each other. "Gnaeus," they said at the same time, and laughed.

"I have an idea," said Lucius. "Logo, you'll need to stay here. Demetria and I will go to Rome."

"What will you do?"

"Follow the *haruspices*, find out where the *baculum* is, and get it back."

::XXV::

Logo was in favor of going to Rome with the youths, but he knew someone had to stay behind and do whatever was necessary to keep the *casula* and the Caves of Egeria secret. They made hasty preparations for Lucius and Demetria to go to Rome.

"Go with the speed of Mercury-- and the stealth of Ulysses," said Logo. "You had better not let anyone see you, if possible. The seers will find out, and they will be ready for you. The only hope is in surprise."

"We will make you proud, dear Logophilus," said Demetria, hugging him tight.

"If only Glyph were here!" said Logo, as he accepted an embrace from Lucius as well.

Demetria and Lucius, both in traveler's clothing and *petasus* hats, walked through the night, arriving at the sacred grove of Numa Pompilius near daybreak. To stay awake, they'd talked and planned, and they began to execute those plans as soon as they were among the oaks.

"I know how to stay out of sight," said Demetria. "I can go into town."

"Gather the boys," said Lucius. "Only the oldest, the most trustworthy. First hour after sunset, here in the grove. And tell them... to bring their slings."

Demetria winked.

It was a cool evening, with broken clouds hiding a rising quarter moon. Several boys appeared with lit torches, which were needed under the dark canopy of pines and oaks in the clearing. They arrived in ones and twos, until there were more than a dozen. Finally, Demetria came with Publius Valerius, the boy who'd called her a brat a few months before.

"Publius, my friend," said Lucius, and clasped him by both hands. Publius showed him his sling, a length of rope with a leather pouch in the middle for a stone. Gnaeus wasn't the only Roman who used a sling-- to hunt birds or just for fun. Now they would be used for a nobler purpose.

"You are not just guarding bark, I think," said Publius. "We did not hear about the departure of the Etruscan seers-- they are very good at keeping secrets-- but when they came back with the *haruspica* burned and ill, the whole city could not stop speaking about what must have happened."

Tullius, one of the older boys at the boy's council that midsummer night, put in, "Demetria has spoken of the power of King Numa's scrolls. Is it true that you melted the mirror of the Etruscan seer? Can you show us?"

The other boys crowded around and shouted similar questions.

Lucius said, "Are Arruns or Sextus here? Where are the kings' sons?"

Someone said, "There is a guard around the house of King Tarquinius. We could not come close. None of the Etruscan boys are here. Their parents are fearful."

Lucius nodded and explained as best he could about the scrolls, grammarstones, and *baculum*, swearing all the boys to secrecy. He told them that the *haruspices* had stolen the *baculum*, and that as Romans they needed to return it to its rightful Roman hands.

"Does anyone know where the *haruspices* are now?"

"We have heard tell they have spent much time in the Temple of Vulcan," said Publius.

"The temple at the foot of Jupiter's hill?" asked Lucius. "Or the one to Sethlans, the Vulcan of the Etruscans, outside Rome?"

"I don't know which one," said Valerius. "All I know is Temple of Vulcan."

Demetria said, "It would be surprising if they were in the Roman temple. Anyway, if we want to go there, it will be difficult at night. We sneaked out of the walls of the city; it is much harder to sneak back in."

Several of the boys stared at Demetria, for girls were not supposed to be part of the boy's council. But she had already proved to them her right to be with the boys by her friendship with Lucius, and her stealthy appearance in Rome. "Sethlans it is, then," said Lucius. "Demetria, stay back with a few of these boys. We will call on you if we need help."

"I don't think so!" she cried.

"You don't have a sling, do you?" said Publius.

Demetria scowled at Publius, but agreed she hadn't one. "That's all right. You three," she said, pointing to the youngest of the bunch. "I have another idea."

Lucius ran, wondering what Demetria had in mind.

The temple of Sethlans was set in a sacred grove similar to that of Numa Pompilius. Italian pines ringed it, and it itself was circular, with twelve pillars on its perimeter that held up a peaked, tiled roof slanting up to a hole for the smoke of the fire of the god to escape. Smoke was rising from the hole, and there was the smell of animal fat; the Etruscans had sacrificed a sheep and looked at its liver to discover the future.

There were twelve thresholds, all built like the *dokana* into the other world.

As they sat there in the bushes, *Haruspices* appeared from each portal, including Turanquil, and stood at each threshold, holding mirrors. Along the side of Turanquil's face was a burn scar, bright maroon, and her ear was deformed.

"They know we're here," said Tullius.

"Of course they do," said Publius. "They checked the omens."

"Throw the stones," said Lucius. "We will see how they like it."

Several boys threw grammarstones from their slings at the *haruspices*. Some of the stones flew over their heads and exploded with a bang on the walls of the temple. Others were intercepted by the mirrors and directed away or back at the boys.

"Ow!" screamed a boy, and fell as a grammarstone hit him on the back of his shoulder.

"Not at the mirrors!" Lucius screamed. "In front, behind, over."

In short order, grammarstones came flying again, but not at

the mirrors. Soon, the *haruspices* retreated inside the temple in a haze of smoke and with the smell of burnt rock.

The boys cheered and ran forward.

Turanquil shouted from inside, "Come no closer or we'll be forced to harm you."

"Who says you can?" jeered one of the boys.

"Stop," said Lucius. "They're right. They can throw daggers, and they rarely miss."

"Your fathers will hear of this," said Turanquil. "You will work long and hard to pay for the damage you've done to this sacred place. And ware the god's wrath, children."

"This is a place of Sethlans," said one of the boys. "Vulcan is our god."

"Quiet! They speak to make you speak, they hear every voice, they know how many we are, and they defend," said Lucius.

"What if our fathers find out?" said one of the boys. "They're right. We'll be badly whipped, I think, and be out in the hot sun cutting rock like slaves to satisfy the god's anger."

"Don't be stupid," said Lucius. "This is the most important thing you have done since you were born. Stay here. I will see what I can see."

Lucius crept close, until he was almost at the pillars. Then he whispered, "*baculum mani magi magistri ventod.*" *The cane in the hand of the master mage by the wind.*

Nothing happened. He crawled behind a pillar and whispered the grammar again.

Nothing.

Then he saw his face, in the face of a mirror.

He shut his eyes, whirled, and kicked up with a foot.

"Ow! By Sethlans!" cursed a *haruspex*.

Lucius had caught the man in the forearm. His mirror went flying. Lucius got up, stepped behind a pillar, and narrowly avoided the thrust of the man's dagger. Then he ducked and ran. A throwing dagger thunked heavily into the pillar, where his head had been a moment ago.

When he got back, Valerius said, "We need to return with swords. They will kill us armed only with these marbles."

"No," said Lucius. "This is our only chance. They will call in the army, and we will be routed, unless we get our hands on the *baculum* tonight."

As Lucius said "army," there was the sound of a little trumpet inside the temple, one familiar to all Romans as the "to my aid" call. The watch on duty would be there in a few minutes, with swords and spears, and that would be the end of the revolution.

"By Hercules! By my genius!" several of the boys groaned. "We are lost."

"Then go," said Valerius. "If you are not willing to give your life for Rome, then we do not need you with us."

A couple of the younger boys said, "We do not even have the *toga virilis* yet."

"That's right, brats. Away with you."

Lucius cried, "Wait! How many grammarstones do you have left?"

Most had one or two, a few five or six.

"Give me them," said Lucius.

He opened his mouth to put as many grammarstones into his mouth as he could. He remembered that first night, when he had seen the stones lodged in the back of the *magus magister*'s throat.

"What do you do?" Valerius said.

"I will make my words powerful as they come from my mouth," said Lucius.

"But that can't work."

"It has. I have seen it done."

"You can't speak with marbles in your mouth," said one of the younger boys.

"He can!" said Tullius. "He has spoken this way before! Practicing to speak before the boys' council."

This quieted the group, because they had all seen Lucius practicing, and knew he was the best speaker of the council.

Lucius took the stones and jammed them into the sides of his mouth and jaw, hoping not to swallow any. He might have had two dozen when he was finished.

"Speak!" Valerius said.

"*Gopp!*" Lucius blurted, and a grammarstone flew out of his mouth.

"Too many!" said Valerius.

"*Bennnest... All's well,*" Lucius said, but he did spit a couple out. "Now. Now I can."

Again, he half-crawled, half-ran to a threshold of the temple. Spying the figure of a *haruspex* lurking there, he said, "*o lucs oculei haruspicis caecans,*" *I summon light in the eye of the soothsayer, blinding.* There was a flash, and the sound of a mirror dropping to the pavement. The *haruspex* bent over double, his hands to his eyes.

Lucius ran to the threshold to get a look. A fire was going in the center of the temple's pavement. The other eleven *haruspices* were at the doors, but had turned to the man, now on his knees and roaring with pain.

"Stay where you are!" yelled Turanquil. "Do not let anyone through your door."

Lucius then saw, on the flat surface of the altar, what looked like the *baculum*, but in the light of the fire it was shinier, reflecting the reddish-gold flame. Next to the *baculum* lay an axe-haft, and a shattered axe blade.

"They tried to destroy it!" Lucius whispered to himself. "They do not want to use its power."

Lucius stood in the threshold, and said, as loudly and clearly as he could, "*O lucs oculeis haruspicum caecantes.*" *I summon light in the eyes of the soothsayers, blinding.*

He gulped on a grammarstone, choked, nearly swallowed. Three went flying out of his mouth.

But the *haruspices* were not blinded.

Had he not spoken clearly?

Six daggers came flying at him. He dived for the threshold, and five of them missed. The sixth glanced his heel, above the ankle. He cursed, rolled, and put his hand to the slash. There was no way he was going to run; pain coursed through him.

Then, as his mind became used to the pain, he realized he had made a mistake in his grammar. *Caecantes* was plural. He had only summoned one light, *O lucs*. His companion did not agree with his namer.

"Once more," he said, trying not to think of the blood staining his sandal.

But he did not have the chance to devise another grammar.

Above, he heard screaming and jeering of boys, and then the explosions of grammarstones.

The courtyard of the temple filled with smoke. A ladder

came down from the hole in the ceiling, and a figure scrambled down the rungs.

Demetria.

"The daggers!" Lucius tried to say, but found the grammarstones had migrated to the middle of his mouth, and he could no longer speak.

Demetria ran, picked up the *baculum* from the altar, and threw it end over end to Lucius. He caught it halfway up, and had it by the short side, with the knob in the air and ready. He flicked the *baculum* to chamber a stone, but there was no click, and in fact, no sound of stones inside it. Was it empty?

"Use the cane!" screamed Demetria, lying face down in front of the altar.

Another round of grammarstones rained down from the ceiling. There was no throwing any daggers now. The smoke was too thick.

Lucius examined the knob. It would not open. Something had been stuffed in the chamber of the cane. There was no way open the knob, much less loose a grammarstone.

"Run!" Lucius said.

They did so, and Lucius limped after them. Once in the shelter of the grove, Demetria noticed his wound, and a boy tore his tunic, and they bound his foot with the rags.

"Brave," said Demetria.

"Braver," said Lucius back to her. "The ladders?"

"I have been to the temple of Sethlans before," Demetria said. "I thought the ladders would come in handy, even if we didn't have slings."

They had hardly gotten on their road back to Rome when they heard the sound of armored men running toward them, their bronze sword-belts jingling in the quiet of the night. There were two dozen of them, some with lit torches, by their insignia a detachment of the king's guard, and they had their swords drawn.

"Stop!" shouted the centurion as they met. "Friend or foe?"

Lucius spoke for them. "Friend, centurion! We need help. The temple of Sethlans-outside-walls is under attack." He pointed. "We tried to defend, but we have no weapons."

"And someone has stolen siege ladders from the armory," said Demetria.

The centurion said, "Who are the attackers?"

"Monsters!" Demetria exclaimed, raising her palms.

"Shut up, little girl," said one of the men.

"See for yourself!"

The centurion adjusted his skullcap. "What are you doing outside the city at night, boys?"

"Defending Rome, sir," said Publius.

The centurion shook his head and said, "Seize these boys-- their parents--"

But a man stood up from behind them, an officer. "Let them go, centurion," he said. "We don't have time to fool with boys when there is an enemy in the sacred grove."

The officer was Marcus Junius.

It was all Lucius could do not to cry out in surprise and joy and astonishment. He ran past his brother, head down, with the other boys. As he left, he turned his head. Marcus nodded at him, then turned away toward the detachment of troops.

Back in the grove, they all gathered around the *baculum*.

"Behold! It is wondrously made," Tullius said with a gasp.

"It is useless," said Lucius. "They have filled it with

something. It can't open anymore."

"We can take out whatever is inside," said Demetria.

"We must go back to Logo," said Lucius. He turned to his allies. "Let's go. All back to your own houses. You know what happened tonight. The city and gods of Rome thank you for your service. I will remember this, when we have overthrown the Etruscans and the rule of the city is ours again. My brother, Marcus Junius, will vouch for all of you."

And they all went their separate ways, leaving the grove of Numa Pompilius.

::XXVI::

The trip back to the *casula* seemed a short one-- they arrived before dawn, with Kaneesh barking up a storm to greet them.

"Thank all the gods," said Logo.

"Thank the God of Everything," said Demetria.

After breakfast, Logo examined the *baculum*. "They have poured molten gold into the hollow and the chamber, locking the grammarstones inside," said Logo. "They must have gotten one of the smiths of Sethlans to do it for them. This is why they brought it there, as a relic for the god."

"After they tried to destroy it with an axe," said Lucius, and described what he had seen next to the altar of Sethlans.

"It would take a lot more to destroy this," said Logo.

"Well, the gold inside means we cannot fly any grammarstones from it. The stones are sealed inside."

"It is well," said Logo. "Do not break the seal of the gold. That is a way we can avoid using it."

"Avoid using it?" Lucius said. "What about the prodigies?" asked Lucius.

214

"As you know, I have learned a few things," said Logo. "I think I will be able to keep the prodigies in check. Especially since the *magus magister* is no longer there to use them for his own ends."

"But cannot we take the gold out? It is for Lucius to use, Logo," said Demetria.

"We could take the gold out," said Logo. "If there were a time of great need. But you need to be wary. The power of the grammarstones is great. Glyph knew how great, but he was wise, and he kept the *baculum* hidden, and the grammarstones with it."

"Lucius would use the power for good-- for the good of Rome," said Demetria.

"As king?" Logo said, and turned to Lucius.

"You said--" Lucius began, and thought hard. "We never could have recovered the *baculum* without the help of my friends. I could never be their king. They are my friends."

Logo grunted his approval.

"So we would need to have... what is it that you called it? A republic. A thing of the people."

"With women-- and Greeks-- as part of the people," said Demetria.

"But first, Tarquin must give up his rule," Logo said.

"He will, because his sons, Sextus and Arruns, are my friends as well, and they will persuade their father."

"Let us hope."

"So," Lucius said. "I guess that means I am not to be a priest of Numa Pompilius anymore?"

"After a year, you must go back anyway, so the king decreed," said Demetria.

"It will be a cold winter, and drafty. Nothing great to be accomplished except spending a lot of time with scrolls and oil lamps. But when the time comes, Kaneesh will miss you," said Logo. "As will I."

"And I?" said Demetria.

"Back home. Your parents are certainly worried. Lucius will be home before you know it."

Lucius thought to himself, *Now I can be married, anyway.* But he said nothing about that. "Does this mean the end of my grammar studies?"

"Not at all," said Logo. "You'll need to study and use the grammar," said Logo. "Perhaps not exactly as it has been used before. But it will be powerful. More powerful than ever we will know."

Demetria and Lucius exchanged glances.

"Let's go, then," said Lucius.

FINIS

GLOSSARY OF LATIN TERMS

If you are a teacher and interested in exploring the themes, cultures, history, and languages of *The Mirror and the Mage* with your students, please visit my website, Breakfast with Pandora Books (http://www.breakfastwithpandora.com) for details on how to obtain a Teacher's Guide and an author visit.

baculum: In Latin, this word means *walking stick* or *cane*. Glyph uses the *baculum* as a walking stick at times in the book. As far as I know, there is no such thing as a magic wand in Roman culture, but the Roman historian Livy notes that Lucius carries a *baculum* made from horn that is filled with gold on the inside.

casula: This is the Latin word for a hut or very small house. Logo's *casula* is one room, big enough for his bed, some storage, and with a space in the middle to stretch out a straw-filled mattress for guests. The *-ula* at the end of the word means "small." In Spanish, which comes from Latin, a regular-sized house is called a *casa*.

companions: The word used by Glyph to designate an adjective. An adjective in Latin is said to "accompany" a noun because it agrees in case, number, and gender.

genius: The genius is a difficult thing to describe exactly, but ancient sources suggest it is kind of spiritual double of oneself, a guardian spirit: yourself, that is, except as a supernatural and helpful being. Demetria would not have had a genius but a *juno*, a female genius. In this book I decided to minimize confusion, especially since some readers know that "Juno" is also the name of a goddess completely different from a *juno*.

haruspex, haruspica, haruspices: A *haruspex* is an Etruscan prophet, soothsayer, seer, and priest who is a man. A *haruspica* is the same type of person, but she's a woman. *Haruspices* designates more than one *haruspex* or *haruspica*. In Etruscan religion, these individuals were in charge of gaining knowledge about present or future situations, especially mysterious ones, by examining livers of animals who had been sacrificed. The *haruspices* in this book have added the ability to use magic by means of their mirrors.

kinds: The word used by Glyph to designate a declension. Declensions are groups of nouns with similar endings, and sometimes, similar gender. There are five declensions in Latin grammar.

magus magister: The word *magus* means magician, and *magister* means master. It can also mean teacher. So a *magus magister* is a master magician, or mage who is skilled enough to teach magic.

neithers (neuter gender): this is a category of grammar in Latin (as well as German) that designates a noun as neither masculine nor feminine.

palla: A article of clothing worn by a Roman woman over her *stola*, or long dress, as a kind of shawl and head-covering.

petasus: This is a Greek word for a wide-brimmed traveler's hat. In addition to helping the wearer conceal his or her identity, it is also useful for keeping the hot Mediterranean sun off one's face, or as a kind of umbrella when it rains.

possibilities: The word used by Glyph to designate a grammatical case in the Latin language. A case is indicated by the ending of a Latin word. In The Mirror and the Mage, there is a different ending for each of the possibilities in their own kind. In the Classical Latin learnt by most schoolchildren now, endings of cases (possibilities) are often repeated in the same declension (kind). There are seven possibilities that have corresponding names in Latin grammar: the *Summoner* (Vocative case); the *Namer* (Nominative case); the *Striker* (Accusative case); the *Bestower* (Dative case); the *Owner* (Genitive case); the *Builder* (Ablative case); and the *Placer* (Locative case).

speculum: This is the Latin word for mirror. The bronze mirrors of Etruscan haruspices in this book are based on mirrors found by archeologists in real Etruscan tombs. Glass mirrors were not in general use at this time; bronze, which is an alloy of tin and copper, was used to create a hand mirror with a long handle (sometimes also bronze, sometimes other materials such as wood) and oval face. One side was the reflecting side, in which you could see your face when the metal was polished. The other side was frequently decorated with a scene from Etruscan or Greek mythology, with names of characters labeled in the Etruscan alphabet.

toga virilis: This is an elaborate robe given to a youth who is officially becoming a man. A toga is a garment used for public business such as court cases, politics, speeches, and voting, and anything else having to do with being a Roman.

DISCUSSION QUESTIONS

1. At the beginning of the story, Lucius decides to swim the Tiber River, even though there is a good chance he will drown. Have you ever done anything you or others considered risky or adventurous? What benefit, gain, reward, or prize was promised if you succeeded, and what would you suffer if you failed? Or was it something you just decided to do for fun or to see what happened? How much did peer pressure contribute to your doing or not doing the act? Is it ever worth it to put yourself at risk to do something?

2. Demetria and Lucius were best friends when they were young children. What is it that makes Lucius decide not to talk to her when he is on his way to see the king? Can you think of a time when you let go of a friend in favor of someone else or another group? What were your reasons at the time? Did you explain them to your friend? Did your friend understand? Consider what you would say to your friend now. Would your message change?

3. From what you read, how much choice do you think Lucius has as to whether he will be a warrior or a priest? Make a list of all the factors involved in coming to his decision. Include other peoples' opinions, what he himself has done toward becoming a priest or a warrior, how his family is involved in the decision, and what he himself wants. Is the

THE MIRROR AND THE MAGE

decision-making process of a Roman teenager any different from that of a modern American? In what ways?

4. If you were Lucius' friend, what would you advise him to decide in becoming a priest or a warrior? Use the list from the previous question to guide your advice of your friend, and take turns making your argument with someone else who has read the book.

5. Lucius goes to the shrine of Numa Pompilius alone. It takes him all day to walk there. How much freedom do your parents give you to get places on your own? Would you rather they give you more or less freedom? What factors do you think made it important for Lucius, in this case, to go alone, rather than being accompanied by his brother, friends, or parents?

6. Let's say you lived in a world where language was not written down. How would life be different from the life you live now? What advantages do letters and words written down give a civilization? How might written language be considered "magic" for those who are not familiar with it?

7. Lucius wants to be able master the *baculum* and the grammarstones right away, but everything takes practice. What have you had to work hard to get good at? Do you spend your time getting good at one or two things, or do you try out a bunch of different things?

8. Do you think that those who end up doing great things succeed because they get lucky, or because they are skilled?

9. When Lucius attempts to defeat the *haruspices* at the house of Celer, he decides to do it on his own. Do you think you would have handled the situation the same way that Lucius did? What would you do different? Are you someone who takes charge of the situation, or do you let others take the lead? What is the difference between being foolish and being brave? Between being independent and knowing when you need help?

10. Given that the Etruscan *haruspices* are not known for attacking actively, but defending, why do you think that the *haruspica* Turanquil threw her knife? Do you think she was aiming at Glyph, or at Lucius?

11. Have you ever had someone close to you die unexpectedly? If they were able to write a letter to you, what would you like it to say? If you could write a letter to that person, what would you say?

12. When you look in the mirror, does it ever feel like there is someone else on the other side of the glass? Do you see how it might be possible for people to believe in a genius based on seeing one's reflection?

13. How do you think looking into a glass mirror is different from looking into a bronze mirror? You can probably get a similar reflection from looking at yourself on the surface of a dark iPad, or on the hood of a dark-colored car. Try looking at yourself in many different reflective surfaces, such as a pool of water, or a stainless steel spoon. How are you

distorted? Create a story about your "double" for each kind of reflection.

14. How creepy is it for you to be alone in the dark? Have you ever been in a place where it's so dark you can't see your hand in front of your face?

15. When someone tells you you're ugly, or makes some other remark that is supposed to cut you down, how do you react? Would you like to react differently?

16. Lucius figured out that the word *dokana* was a "neither" rather than female, and he was able to perfect his grammar. Think of a time when you really had to put your mind to solving a problem. What was the "breakthrough" or "aha!" moment?

17. What do you think is going to happen to Lucius and Demetria? Will they be married someday? In Roman society, Greeks and Romans tended not to get married. Why do you think that is?

18. What do you think is going to happen to the *baculum* now that its grammarstone shaft is filled with gold?

ACKNOWLEDGMENTS

I have dedicated *The Mirror and the Mage* to my teachers, without whom it would never have been possible, and I give hearty and humble thanks to them, and especially to the four who affected me most profoundly: Mrs. Linda Mengel and Mrs. C. Adeline D. ("Addie") Holsing, encouragers of a young writer; Professor Doris Betts, mentor of an older writer; and Mrs. Mary Small-- a better Latin teacher there has never been in the history of the world. Thanks also to Janet Purvis, Sherry Jankowski, Ashlie Canipe, Peggy Swearingen, Neville Sinclair, and Richard Abbott, who read the book in manuscript and gave invaluable feedback, aid, and encouragement. I thank also my writing comrades Lyn Hawks, my partner at True North Writers & Publishers Co-operative, and again Richard Abbott, who has helped me bring my vision of Rome to the digital age. Finally, to my family, and especially my wife Celeste, who remains my beacon in the stormy sea of writing and publishing in the twenty-first century. *Gratias ago vobis omnibus.* Thanks-- everyone.